FROM LONDON, WITH LOVE

BEC MCMASTER

For my readers.

London Steampunk would only ever have been a glimmer in my eye, if not for your support.

This one is for you.

CHAPTER 1

The queen was not amused.

In fact, the Duke of Malloryn was counting on it.

"What do you mean by 'we need to discuss succession plans'?" she repeated, in a very clear, very precise voice that may have made others quiver.

Malloryn eased back in his chair, feeling the weight of seven pairs of eyes coming to rest upon him. The Council of Dukes had come together to discuss the rebuilding of parliament following the bombing of the Ivory Tower, and he'd managed to throw in this little agenda item at the last moment.

It was hardly unplanned.

"Precisely that, Your Majesty," he said. "You have no legitimate heir, and Lord Balfour came awfully close to killing you six months ago—"

"He failed," she snapped.

"You're not invincible, Your Majesty." He caught a glimpse of several of the other councilors exchanging glances —most notably the Duchess of Casavian and her husband, Lord Barrons. They'd be two of the more important ones to convince. Mina was the queen's dearest friend—and loudest supporter—and if he didn't have her vote, then the queen might escape his latest ploy. "We've spent the last dozen or so years trying to overthrow a tyrant. We succeeded, but weeding out the last of his supporters has taken some doing. For the first time in... God, over a century, London has peace, but it's so newly forged and you are the figurehead of that peace. If something happens to you, then it shall be war again. I'm tired of war. I want to take a bloody holiday with my wife without the palace going up in flames. And as much as none of us would like to discuss the unthinkable, the truth remains: You have no heir."

Only several bastard cousins who would squabble over the crown like a pack of bloody magpies.

"And since you have no intentions of marrying and providing one, something must be done. You must name one of your cousins as your heir."

"My cousins are illegitimate," she replied through clenched teeth. "And the Countess of Drewsbury went to great lengths to produce a forged marriage certificate between her grandparents in an attempt to place herself on my throne all those years ago. I will burn the damned throne before I let her sit on it."

He leaned forward, trying not to smile now she'd taken the bait. "You have other cousins."

"Eugene?" The queen's voice rose. "He's an idiot. And his sister, Imogen, would be the one pulling his strings."

"While we can agree on the first," he pointed out, "I doubt Princess Imogen would be the one in command."

Queen Alexandra's eyes narrowed. "A regency, Malloryn? We've already had one of those, and it ended badly."

"Eugene's your best option. If something happened, he'd be declared *non compos*, and a regent appointed."

"Imogen would never allow it."

He merely crossed his palms over his middle and arched a brow. "Accidents happen, Your Majesty."

"You are *not* going to murder my cousin, no matter how greedy and grasping she may be," the queen said, pushing to her feet and slamming both hands on the table. "And you are *not* going to sit that idiot on my throne."

Excellent. His lashes hooded over his eyes. "You won't marry. You won't provide an heir. You won't name an heir. What are we meant to do, Alexandra?"

The queen's lips pressed together firmly. She was so bloody stubborn, and while he could understand her aversion to marriage, the realm didn't have the luxury of it.

"I see," she said coldly. "All this talk of heirs. Of Eugene. Of Imogen. This all bloody goes back to marrying me off, doesn't it?" Then she laughed. "You want me to marry, and if the halter won't work, then the prod might. I can't believe I actually thought you were seriously thinking my cousin might be a potential king." She stabbed a finger in the air. "Don't think you can fool me. I know exactly what you're up to, Malloryn."

He allowed a faint smile. *I quite doubt it.*

Help came from an unexpected source. "As much as you dislike the idea, Alexandra," Mina, the Duchess of Casavian, murmured, "Malloryn does speak the truth. There have been several assassination attempts on you in the past year alone. We can wrap you in a suit of armor, we can guard you day and night, we can do everything we can to protect you, but all it will take is one stray bullet and England will be facing another civil war."

The queen looked at her dearest friend with an aghast expression. "*You* want me to marry?"

Mina looked up, and it was clear something silent was exchanged between them. "Some of us do not have the luxury of forgoing such alliances," she said softly. "But this time, the choice will be yours. This time, the power will be yours. This time, your husband need only be a consort in truth."

The queen quivered with suppressed fury as she cut the room a sharp glance. "And the rest of you?"

Lynch, the Duke of Bleight, looked troubled. "I've been on those streets and I've seen civil war up close. The potential to return to those days is simply too great a risk. I must concur with Malloryn, Your Majesty."

"As do I," said his wife, Rosalind.

Leo Barrons drummed his fingers on the table, his gaze slanting toward his wife, even as his face remained impassive. "In this instance, I agree with my wife."

Malloryn turned to the remaining two council members.

"I ain't one to force a lady where she ain't want to go," Blade replied, tipping his head toward the queen. "So it's a no from me."

"And a no from me too," Sir Gideon snapped.

Four votes to two.

The queen could override them if she chose—the power was ultimately hers—but she rarely, if ever, did so.

"Rot you, Malloryn." The queen tipped her chin up haughtily, then swept her skirts behind her. "If I am forced to take another husband, then so be it. But I shall be damned if it is one of your choosing. I will make my decision by the end of midsummer. Send whatever invitations you wish, trot out your prospective suitors, wine and dine your foreign princes..., but the choice will be mine."

"I would never expect anything else," he conceded, feeling the faint stir of victory shiver through him.

It was done.

And perhaps, when this was all over, she'd forgive him.

But right now, she swept from the room, her shoulders squared as if she faced a firing squad and her face as stony as he'd ever seen it.

Malloryn released the breath he'd been holding. Excellent. The first roll of the die had been cast, the game now afoot. He only had to maneuver the last little piece into place.

And right on cue....

"You play a dangerous game, Malloryn," said Sir Gideon Scott, pushing his chair back with a squeal. "Didn't our last prince consort do enough damage for you?"

Malloryn schooled his features, and deliberately quirked a brow. "Perhaps the queen will finally find happiness? Do you not wish that for her?"

Sir Gideon's eyes narrowed. "Of course, I wish for my queen's happiness. But forcing her into another marriage, when she's barely recovered from the ordeal of her last one? It seems nothing short of cruel."

"Ah, now, Sir Gideon," Malloryn chided. "Not all marriages are prisons. Some are quite joyful."

"Did he just say marriage was joyful?" Barrons joked to Mina. "I fear Malloryn may have been inserted with that mind-controlling chip that Lord Balfour was using last summer. Quick. Someone shock him with a stunner to see if we can short-circuit it."

"If anyone comes near me with a stunner, then I'll shove it up their—"

"This is no joking matter." Sir Gideon still seemed flushed. "Perhaps you should see to her," Sir Gideon suggested to the Duchess of Casavian, his voice softening a little.

Mina winced.

"I should," she said, "though she may not welcome my presence just yet, after I voted against her wishes." The duchess's brow furrowed in misery. "Perhaps it would be best if *you* went after her, Sir Gideon? You were the one to vote no."

"Blade also—"

"Think she ain't wantin' to see my sorry mug," Blade said bluntly. "I don't mince around the palace much. You're 'er friend, ain't you?"

Sir Gideon glanced toward the door, then cast Malloryn one last dark look. "She won't forgive you for this."

Malloryn merely shrugged. "I think she will."

The door swung shut behind Sir Gideon.

Silence reigned in the council chambers, and Malloryn deliberately refused to meet anyone else's eyes.

"You're playin' dangerous games," Blade said, pushing to his feet. "You sure it's gonna end well for you?"

Malloryn merely smiled. "I think I'll be forgiven once all is said and done. They just need... a nudge."

"YOUR MAJESTY."

The queen paused in the hallway, closing her eyes briefly against the stab of pain that lit through her chest. Just a single moment of grief before she resumed the mantle of the throne. Sweeping her face clean of expression, she turned to confront her tormentor.

"Sir Gideon," she replied.

He strode toward her, his face stern. "I'm sorry. I tried."

"That's quite all right," she murmured as he paused five feet away from her. "You are only one voice. And Malloryn is clearly pursuing an agenda, if he has the rest of them in his pocket."

"Apart from Blade."

"Sir Henry votes as he wishes," Alexandra murmured. It was one of the reasons she enjoyed having him on the council. It was, as Sir Henry would have said, like setting the cat among the pigeons.

Or some grammatically slaughtered version of that sentence.

Silence fell across the pair of them like a shroud.

She hated these sudden lingering silences.

Once upon a time, they might have shared a certain period of quietness, simply enjoying the pleasure of each other's company, but ever since her sojourn at Sir Gideon's country manor six months ago, the quiet seemed filled with all the memories they dared not speak of.

"I think—"

"You can overrule them—"

They both stared at each other.

Sir Gideon tried again. "You're the queen. You're the only one who can override a council vote. If you don't wish to marry, then that option is entirely yours."

Alexandra turned to the window, staring down at the vast gardens of Kensington Palace. "I could," she admitted softly. The second they'd cast the vote, it was what all her instincts had urged her to do. Cast the vote back in Malloryn's smug face and let him choke on it. But she was the queen. She was England, damn it. And while the woman's heart that beat in her chest wanted to hit something, the part of her that was a queen had to look at the proposition from all angles. "But Malloryn does have a point."

England deserved better than the current instability of the realm, with no named heir and a handful of illegitimate cousins and power-hungry nobles waiting in the background to pursue a claim. Her realm had suffered so much more than she ever had, and she owed her people a stable, secure future.

No more civil wars. No more brutality and uncertainty.

If she was to truly forge the future she wanted for her people, then she would have to swallow down one more indignity.

"Malloryn's going to drown you in potential suitors," he warned.

She snorted. "Don't think him a fool. Malloryn's already chosen my future husband, I'll bet my life upon it. He doesn't gamble unless he's got a certain hand."

Sir Gideon's lips thinned. "A foreign prince, no doubt."

"No doubt."

It made sense to forge strong ties with another country,

but she hated the way he could speak of it with such composure.

"Then I shall wish you luck," Sir Gideon murmured. "I hope he's someone you can forge a friendship with, in the least."

The queen agreed.

But the woman inside her wanted to lash out.

Is that all you have to say to me? Good luck?

Can you not be just the slightest bit angry about it all? Or... jealous?

But that was not Sir Gideon's way.

Especially not after the incident at Haver Hall.

Those lips had found hers ardently in the conifer maze in his gardens. If she pressed her fingertips to her mouth, she thought she might still be able to feel the tingle.

It had been a moment of madness—for both of them. Good sense giving way to desire, all the unconfessed yearnings of her heart spilling out of her like a torrent of need. And his touch, God, his touch.... So gentle, so reverent.... Until passion swept them both away, and Sir Gideon had pushed her back against the stone wall of the folly, pinning her wrists there.

Instantly, desire had faded.

That moment had taken her back into the past, and suddenly it wasn't Sir Gideon's mouth on hers, but the tainted memory of her husband's dead fish lips—taking, consuming, demanding.

She'd fought her way free, and it was only then she realized she was in Sir Gideon's garden, with the man himself—rather than enslaved by a ghost.

Sir Gideon had been horrified and apologized profusely. And the moment of madness had ended, leaving the pair of them in this never-ending dance of politeness and aloof silences.

"Friendship," she whispered. Once upon a time, she might

have wished for more, but she was no longer that foolish young princess. "Yes. Hopefully I may find friendship, at least."

Sir Gideon bowed his dark head. "I'll take my leave then, Your Majesty. I only came to ensure you were not upset."

"Thank you."

"You're welcome." He seemed to hesitate, as if there was something else he wished to say, but then the moment was lost.

And he was striding away from her, his broad shoulders straight and the edge of his dark hair tumbling to his collar, always a half inch in need of a trim. Her fingers seemed to constantly itch to stroke through it.

But she was the queen.

She could not afford to be a woman, especially one who yearned, no matter how much she wished to.

"Curse you, Malloryn," she whispered. "Curse you."

CHAPTER 2

It was an intricately plotted affair.

It ought to have been. The Duke of Malloryn had organized the entire thing.

The first ball of what Malloryn was affectionately calling "the husband hunt" commenced with a quadrille. Foreign dignitaries and princes abounded. Epaulets gleamed. Bludwein spilled into elegant flutes. And through it all, the queen reigned with a smile on her face that never once touched her eyes.

"She's hating every minute of it," said a soft voice at his side.

"She's doing her duty," he replied.

His wife's gilt hair gleamed beneath the light of a dozen chandeliers as Adele laid her gloved hands on the balcony and surveyed the ballroom. "As you did once, when you married me. Hopefully this ends the same way—with the queen desperately in love with her husband. And the favor returned by the groom."

"Desperately? That's a little gauche, is it not?" he teased. "I'm a duke. I do nothing 'desperately.'"

"Considering I had you on your very knees in the rubble

of the Ivory Tower, my love"—Adele cocked a haughty brow—"'desperately' is the precise term I would use."

"Ah." He couldn't suppress a smile. "And how many times are you going to remind me of that proposal? I had *one* moment of weakness—brought about by the emotion of finally thwarting my nemesis, no doubt—and you've thrown it in my face ever since."

"Every day," she promised. "For the rest of my life."

Malloryn stroked his finger and thumb down a golden curl that spilled over her shoulder, twirling it idly around his finger. He'd seen the marriages of his companions and had once thought them a combination of physical chemistry conspiring to lure the unsuspecting to their doom. He'd even succumbed to such madness himself, though he hadn't realized affection held just as much weight as lust in bringing a man to his knees. Every day with Adele by his side brought new revelations—including the fact he'd never have thought to enjoy teasing her so much.

"I think you like seeing me kneeling as penitent before you."

Adele turned her face, biting his finger with a challenge in her eyes. "If you're a nice husband and promise me a waltz tonight, I may return the favor."

His finger stilled. *Jesus.* "Then I shall promise you all of my waltzes tonight."

"Just one, Malloryn," she said with an impish smile as she disengaged his finger from her hair and then twirled away. "Perhaps you should offer the queen one of your others. Save her from her misery."

"I don't think seeing me will rouse any joy in her. I'm currently at the top of a list of people she would care to avoid at the moment."

"I disagree." Adele shrugged, her gaze sliding across the room to where a tall, taciturn man scowled into his wine and very carefully did not look anywhere in the queen's direction.

"I think she might be concentrating on avoiding someone else, to be honest. I daresay you're merely an annoying gnat at her ankle."

"A gnat, am I?" And to think that once upon a time, princes and kings had cowered when he arched an icy eyebrow in their direction. He shook his head as he turned for the stairs. "Sometimes I think you consider it your prime duty in life to keep me humble."

Adele's twinkling laughter filled his ears as he made his way down to the ballroom.

It took him half a minute to intercept the queen, holding out a hand. "May I?"

Alexandra arched a brow, but gracefully accepted, and he swung her into the waltz. "Pleased with yourself?"

"It's your ball," he replied. "I think you should be the one graced with congratulations. The blud-wein is an excellent vintage, everyone seems to be enjoying themselves, and you certainly seem not to lack for dance partners."

"It appears word has gotten around that I seek a consort. I cannot imagine how that happened."

"Neither can I," he replied smoothly. "Though I did invite half of Europe's eligible bachelors to attend the exhibition, so perhaps some of them are merely ambitious and reading between the lines."

"Ah," Alexandra said with a bitter little twist of her lips. "And which one do you care for, Malloryn? I see we have some Russian Blood princes, all with ties to the tsarina. But you don't want me to choose one of them. The Blood play by their own rules, and you'd never be able to control one of them."

"True," he admitted. "Nor would you accept one. They're merely here to keep up appearances. Besides, I have some interest in business with one of the princes. That's why they're here."

"One of the princes?" She scanned the crowd. "Ivan

Feodorovich? What business could you possibly have with him?"

"It's personal," Malloryn told her.

"Malloryn," she warned. "You don't do personal."

"I am merely tying up some loose ends from that entire ordeal in Russia," he assured her. He suddenly smiled. "And I may need a friendly Russian prince one day."

"Always meddling, Malloryn."

"Always," he promised.

She returned her attention to the crowd. "So it's not one of the Russians. I see we have a few swarthy Hapsburgs, but you disapprove of their means of leashing verwulfen."

"I disapprove of collars in general."

"And it cannot be one of the verwulfen candidates—not with the risk I might contract the loupe and die. So the Scandinavians are off the list. And the Spanish are only here for appearances, what with their ties to New Catalan and the Illumination. I daresay you wouldn't want those policies polluting London." She pursed her lips. "Hmm. I daresay you wish to promote blue blood interests in the wake of the revolution. Too many humans on the council and the throne. Time to balance the accounts. Which leaves me with the blue blood candidates from London. Of course. The rest are a distraction. You're trying to screen your ideal candidate from me."

He gave her a considering look. "The choice is yours, Alexandra. I merely offer a buffet from which to consider your options."

"If you think I don't know that you've already chosen my husband, then you either consider me a fool, or a queen who doesn't know her spymaster well enough."

It provoked a laugh. "You've never been a fool." He'd have never been able to help her and the Duchess of Casavian overthrow her husband if she was. "I shall concede: Yes, I've already chosen your husband." Capturing her hand, he pressed a kiss to the back of it. "But I doubt you'll ever guess who."

The queen's eyes narrowed. "So be it, Malloryn. Let the games begin."

And she waded into the melee with her head held high, astutely studying the crowd of suitors.

Malloryn gestured to one of the servants, taking a small snifter of brandy as he watched the queen laugh and placate, and search for his ideal candidate.

A year ago, he'd have never even considered Sir Gideon.

The man was humble and honest and alarmingly human, with a humans first agenda. He was also the sentimental choice, and Malloryn had never held truck with sentiment.

Until recently.

Adele had shown him the error of his ways.

The queen deserved to be happy. She deserved a husband who would cherish her and help her steer the monarchy into a safe, secure future for humans, verwulfen, and blue bloods alike. And Sir Gideon could be reasoned with.

And then, catching the eye of Sir Gideon Scott, who was watching proceedings with a thinly disguised look of irritation on his face, he lifted his glass as if in mutual celebration.

DUKES. PRINCES. BARONS. COUNTS.

Alexandra was starting to lose track of them all. Her cheeks ached from smiling, and her head swam from the reek of perfume and cologne. She circled the ballroom in the arms of a Russian prince, wishing she could be elsewhere.

The choice of dance partner didn't suit her either.

Prince Ivan Feodorovich was too tall and physically imposing. He'd taken her in hand as if she was a prize to be claimed, and though he was perfectly polite, his cool skin unnerved her.

He reminded her a little of her former husband with the hawkish glint in those eyes and the sheer overwhelming masculinity that oozed off him. Though his smile was warmer, she nonetheless felt hunted.

She couldn't breathe.

Her stays... pressing tighter. Constricting all the breath from her lungs.

"Are you well?" he demanded in his thick accent, his hand tightening on her waist. "You seem breathless. Do you wish for fresh air?"

Not with you.

But it was the perfect opportunity. Alexandra made her excuses and discreetly slipped from the ballroom, her skin crawling. She made her way toward her private apartments in a flurry of silk, barely aware of the Coldrush guard and servant who followed her.

Once inside her drawing room, Alexandra pressed her back to the door, closing her eyes and breathing slowly. It was ridiculous. The man had barely touched her, barely even looked at her, yet she'd felt the prickle of nerves alight within her like a sudden sickness.

It was because he was attractive.

Demanding.

Physically imposing.

And worse, a blue blood.

She was the queen of England. No man could control her ever again.

But no matter how often she told herself that, it didn't still the jump of nerves.

How was she going to do this? How was she going to let another man into her bed, when she could barely even stand to be touched?

The only man she felt comfortable around was Sir Gideon, and even then she'd had... a moment. And she'd been kissed once by the Duke of Goethe, before her husband had him murdered. It had been nice, though to be perfectly honest, she'd fallen for Manderlay's quiet charms and his gift of poetry, rather than being swayed physically. And the kiss had been so perfunctory, it hadn't threatened her.

But she trusted Sir Gideon. He felt nonthreatening, and indeed, she'd wanted him to kiss her, once upon a time.

She still wanted him to kiss her, though she doubted he'd ever chance such an encounter again after she'd fled from him that last time.

Indeed, he was possibly the only man of her acquaintance whom she could even consider... lying with.

An idea occurred.

It was ludicrous. Preposterous.

But what if it worked?

Alexandra froze. What if all she needed was frequent exposure with someone she trusted? What if she could defeat this... this fear within her?

"Don't you even think about it," she whispered in the stillness of her rooms.

And yet, the thought of Sir Gideon kissing her again was almost its own type of lure.

And you are *the queen.*

Ava winced as the frequency transmitter squealed. Gemma must have been standing too close to the orchestra.

She swiftly turned the dial for Gemma's communication device down, and scanned through the other Rogues' frequencies. All was well.

The door behind her opened.

"I'm sorry, this room is taken." Ava glanced behind her, then abruptly straightened and dipped a curtsy. "Your Majesty. My apologies. I had no idea it was you. Forgive me."

She'd taken over one of the queen's antechambers for the night, with Malloryn's blessing.

The queen smiled. "Forgiven, Miss McLaren. Whatever are you doing out of bed?"

Ava relaxed. "Oh, I volunteered. Someone has to keep them all in line," she joked, gesturing to the transmitter. And it wasn't as if she was going to be getting much sleep, what with the incessant ache in her hips.

"I trust you are well?" The queen's face softened as she glanced down, though her eyes bore the stain of sadness.

Ava should have been in confinement. No amount of ruffles in the world could conceal the bulk of her midriff, where Kincaid's baby kicked morning and night. But Herbert was the only other person who knew how to work the switchboard, and he was currently enjoying a weekend in Bath with his wife.

"Tolerably well, Your Majesty."

"Malloryn's not working you too hard?"

"Oh no," she hastened to reassure her queen. "He wanted me to rest, but there's no rest to be had, unfortunately. I may as well keep my mind and body busy."

"Oh, I remember those days," the queen murmured, one hand resting on her flat midriff.

Ava stiffened. Oh, no. She'd completely forgotten. The queen's only child had been stillborn. It was the worst thing she could imagine. "I'm so sorry—"

"Don't be." There was no emotion in the queen's eyes, though her lips curled in a placating smile. "Edward's memory should always be kept alive."

Awkwardness fell upon the pair of them, however, and Ava couldn't help bringing a hand to rest upon her swollen abdomen. She'd been cursing the way the baby kicked all night, but she would never take such gestures for granted again.

But what should she say?

"I should get back to the ball," the queen murmured, as if sensing Ava's distress. "Malloryn will be wondering where I am."

"I hope you find someone," Ava called as Her Majesty turned toward the door. "I hope he makes you happy."

The queen glanced over her shoulder. "You're very kind."

Through the door, Ava heard the *whirr* of a servant drone sensing movement and rolling toward the queen.

Accepting a glass of cordial from the drone's tray, the queen swished past, heading toward the ballroom in a cloud of perfume, cordial and something else, something bitter—

Ava's head turned unerringly.

That smell....

The scent of lilacs and oils was almost overwhelming, but her sense of smell was stronger now she was with child—as all scents seemed to be—and she'd know it anywhere.

Ava lumbered toward the drone, grabbing the second flute of champagne and sniffing it.

Bitter almonds. Cyanide. An impressive dose of it.

The cordial!

The doors swung shut behind the queen, and Ava lunged after her, hampered by both her skirts and her bulk. She shoved the doors open, but the queen was vanishing toward the second gallery. Two guards stood side by side at the next set of doors, but it was the elegant brunette pacing in front of a painting that drew her attention. Gemma had drawn guard duty for the night.

"Gemma!" she cried, meeting her friend's eyes from across the room. "The cordial!"

Gemma's smile faded in an instant. Her gaze tracked Ava's, and she leapt toward the queen.

Even as Ava watched, the queen laughed at something a guard had said and lifted the glass to her lips.

There was nothing she could do, nothing she could say—

FROM LONDON, WITH LOVE

And then Gemma slammed into the queen, sending the glass flying, and the pair of them toppling.

Instantly, a cry went up. Guards swarmed out of nowhere, swallowing the pair of them whole.

"What the hell is going on here?" The captain of the guards demanded, as several Coldrush guards hauled Gemma off the queen.

Ava finally fought her way through. "The cordial smells like cyanide!"

The captain helped the queen to her feet, and someone handed her the crown, which had gone flying. The queen shot Gemma a pale-faced look—and Ava couldn't help remembering how long it had taken Her Majesty to forgive Gemma for trying to kill her when she'd been implanted with the mind-controlling chip.

"It's the cordial," she begged the queen. "I smelled it as you went past me. I think it's poisoned."

Malloryn appeared out of nowhere, tucking Gemma under one arm and giving Ava a curt nod to retreat. "I'll handle it," he said to the waiting guards, visibly inspecting the queen. "Did you drink any of it?"

The queen looked shocked. "A sip, perhaps."

"I think you should retire," he stressed.

The queen nodded, and Malloryn gestured for the captain of the guards to escort her to her private rooms.

"Ava," he said.

"I'll gather the evidence," she replied, slipping a small leather satchel from one of the pockets in her gown and withdrawing a sample vial.

She found little enough of the cordial to test, but as she brought her damp fingers to her nose to sniff it, she realized she'd been right.

Someone had poisoned the queen's cordial.

CHAPTER 3

"What the hell do you mean, she was poisoned?" Sir Gideon demanded, pushing his way through the doors into the queen's antechambers despite the burly mech standing on duty outside.

Malloryn captured his forearm, but Gideon was having none of it.

Grabbing the duke by his collar, he shoved him into the wall, searching for Alexandra. "Where is she, damn you? What happened? Have you sent for the doctor, or the—?"

"Sir Gideon. That's enough."

Alexandra. *There*. His breath eased in his chest as the queen pushed to her feet from the chair by the window. Moonlight painted silver *fleur de lis* across the patterns of her gown, but she looked whole and hearty, and as well as he'd ever seen her.

"You weren't poisoned?" he gasped.

"Evidently." Malloryn pried Gideon's clenched fists off his collar. "You're lucky I like you. That cravat took a half hour to knot."

Damn it. He let the bastard go, scrubbing at his mouth. Malloryn could have handed him his teeth, and they both knew it. "You're lucky I trust you with the queen's continued health."

Malloryn arched a cool brow. "I wasn't aware the queen's health was of your particular concern."

"Of course, it's of my concern," he countered, though heat flushed through his cheeks. The words were dangerously close to the truth he tried to hide every damned time he looked at her. "It's of concern to all the council. All of London."

"And yet, none of them are barging into her private chambers like a Suffolk bull given a glimpse of a red rag."

"That's enough," Alexandra repeated. "The both of you." Her voice softened. "Gideon, I'm fine. Luckily, one of Malloryn's agents scented the cyanide in the cordial, and another one of them knocked it from my hand before I could drink much of it."

He couldn't help crossing toward her, though he paused at the edge of the carpet. A decent five feet of distance. "Do we know who it was?"

"No," she murmured. "Malloryn's agents are attempting to find us some answers. It could be anyone. There are so many foreign dignitaries here, anyone could have seized the chance."

"That makes little sense. Half of them are here to… to meet you." He couldn't say the words. "Who would wish you dead?"

Before a potential wedding?

"Someone who would enjoy seeing England cast into chaos," she said. "The French, perhaps? An unruly member of one of the foreign parties? Someone with a grudge against a potential suitor? One of the Echelon who hasn't yet forgiven me for changing the nature of London?"

"Do we have a suspect?"

"Everyone in the castle," Malloryn replied, "aside from myself and my agents, the queen, a handful of guards under lockdown, and yourself. Who told you she'd been poisoned? I was under the impression we'd managed to keep it quiet."

Gideon thought back to the ballroom. "The queen had been gone for half an hour. Then the rumor started circulating. I heard it from Lady Baumbury."

"Interesting. Especially considering I and my agents were the only ones with that knowledge."

Gideon looked at him sharply. "You think someone's slipped up?"

"I think that if I find the source of that rumor, I'll find someone who knows something they shouldn't."

Malloryn's thin smile set the hair on the back of his neck on end.

Sometimes he forgot just how dangerous the duke was. Malloryn wore a thin veneer of civility at all times, but there were claws and teeth beneath the polish, and the cool gleam in those gray eyes was never short of calculating.

"What do you want me to do?' Gideon demanded.

Malloryn turned, cutting a swift glance toward the queen before his lips thinned. "Guard her. With your life, if need be."

"Always," he pledged fervently.

"I'm sure that's hardly necessary," Alexandra broke in. "Sir Gideon has his own affairs to attend to. And I am surrounded by an entire coterie of loyal guards and servants."

Gideon looked down, the swirls in the rug capturing his attention. He couldn't trust himself to look at her in this moment, not without Malloryn seeing the truth in his eyes.

The incident at Haver Hall hovered between them.

He'd kissed her and she'd shoved him away, fright filling those dark eyes. He had pushed too far—taken far more than a mere gentleman like him was owed—and she had pushed back, and quite rightly.

He had tried to be the epitome of restraint and politeness

ever since, but the ghost of that encounter lingered between them every damned time they were in a room together.

"If there is poison in the castle, then we cannot trust even the servants," Malloryn said. "One member of the council must be with you at all times."

"Sir Gideon is human," she protested. "He won't even be able to smell poison."

"No," Malloryn admitted, "but he is emphatically loyal, and while he and I may disagree on several matters of the realm, I trust him with your life." Malloryn tipped his head toward Gideon with a wry smile. "I say that about very few people."

"Malloryn—"

The duke simply strode toward the door, ignoring her, as he was wont to do at times. He fetched his cane. "I don't care what personal grievance the pair of you have at the moment." He gave her a stern look. "You have a responsibility to the realm to keep yourself alive and bloody safe, and you will obey my instructions in this. Stay with Sir Gideon until we can sweep Kensington and discover who put cyanide in your cordial."

"Malloryn—!"

The door swung shut behind the duke.

And then they were alone.

"Curse that blackhearted bastard." The queen balled her hands into fists. "How dare he walk away? How dare he!"

But she didn't respond to the hint Malloryn had thrown into the room like a live bomb.

Sir Gideon waited for half a minute, until he was certain Malloryn would be out of hearing distance. When he looked at her face, he couldn't help catching his breath, for she looked like every single one of his dreams, molded into flesh.

And just like a dream, he feared his hopes toward her would evaporate if he ever dared reach out and touch her again.

"You will be safe, Alexa."

"You shouldn't call me that," she said tartly.

He gave a sad little shrug. "Safe from everything—including my attentions." At the sight of her startled look, he headed toward the door. Best to set matters straight before she worked herself into a state of nerves. Though she'd never said a word about the encounter, they hadn't been alone in a room together ever since. "I'll ring for some tea. I daresay it's going to be a long night."

CHAPTER 4

"What have you got for me?" Malloryn demanded as he entered the makeshift headquarters the Company of Rogues had commandeered at Kensington Palace.

"Tea, Your Grace," Charlie said, handing him a cup of bloodied tea.

"Not precisely what I had in mind." He took a sip regardless. "Gemma?"

The entire membership of COR was gathered around the table. Gemma lounged at the head, looking as though she'd singlehandedly broken the hearts of everyone in the court that night. Leadership suited her. And so did love. It cast a glow across her features that he'd never seen her wear before.

"We've questioned the maids who handled the tea service," Gemma replied, her shoulders squaring. "I'm fairly certain the pair of them had nothing to do with the poisoning. One is absolutely distraught at the thought, and the other has been in the queen's service since she was on short strings. She's so emphatically loyal to the queen, I thought she was going to throw me through the window at the mere suggestion she'd had a hand in it."

He glanced at Obsidian, who nodded.

"Both maid's emotional reactions rang true," the former assassin said. "It's too easy. It's not the maids. They'd be the first to be suspected."

"Who else had access to the queen's antechamber?"

Gemma started listing members of the royal household.

"Your Grace?" Ava lifted her hand. Though she was rapidly approaching the birth of her first child, it had done nothing to hamper her effectiveness as an investigator.

"Yes?"

"I suspect our poisoner isn't an expert."

Ava only ever spoke when she was certain of the evidence. "Go on."

"Firstly, there were several of the queen's favorite lemon cakes on the tray, which were also laced with cyanide. Sugar seems to dull the effect cyanide has on a body. A good poisoner would know that. Her cordial is also sweet. I haven't finished analyzing how much cyanide was laced within the drink, but why risk diluting its effects?"

"Hmm." He rubbed at his jaw. "Interesting. What else?"

"Barrons said rumor began circulating throughout the ball barely half an hour after the queen removed to her rooms following her dance. Alexandra said she couldn't have spent more than fifteen or twenty minutes refreshing herself before she returned to the antechamber where Ava was waiting," Gemma added.

It was a little eerie how well-aligned their thought processes were. Though he *had* completed her training. "Sir Gideon mentioned the same."

"Which gives us a ten-minute window between the queen accepting the cordial and rumor spreading." Gemma's eyes narrowed. "Only the guards witnessed my assault on the queen, and you had the room locked down."

"So there was either someone watching—our poisoner, we may presume," Byrnes broke in, "or someone in the ballroom was aware of what was about to happen."

"Obsidian and I will reinvestigate the queen's antechamber to see if there are any hidden niches one can observe from." Gemma pushed away from the table. "Byrnes, I want you and Charlie pursuing the kitchens lead. Find that cyanide for me." She seemed to notice Malloryn was still there. "Unless Your Grace has another preference?"

He waved her away. "You're in command."

She arched a brow. "I hate you sometimes."

"You were born for this role," he replied. "And I enjoy seeing you in action."

"Fine." Gemma brushed nonexistent lint from her sleeve. "Then I'm going to set you and your wife into action too. None of us can question the occupants of the ballroom. Foreign princes aren't likely to respond to servants like us—"

"I ain't a fuckin' servant," Kincaid growled.

"In their eyes you may as well be," Malloryn murmured. He nodded. "Sir Gideon heard the rumor from Lady Baumbury. I'll set Adele upon her and see if we can trace these whispers back to their source. Anything else, my Lady Rogue?"

Gemma stuck her tongue out at him. "Don't tempt me."

"My search has been unfruitful," Adele told him several hours later as she dumped her reticule on the table. "Lady Baumbury heard it from the Countess of Wessex, who heard of it from Lady Hendricks, who was in a circle of ladies when it was first mentioned, though she cannot recall where it originated from."

"Which ladies?" Malloryn murmured.

Adele pinched the bridge of her nose. "Lady Boxden, Princess Imogen of York, two of the Russians—though Lady Hendricks mangled their names so badly I couldn't confirm their identities—and Lady Abagnale."

"Hmm." He eased away from the table. Rumors were difficult to trace, though Adele had done better than he expected. "There are five female members of the Blood court here in London currently."

"You favor the Russians?"

"Lady Boxden is a wealthy widow who lost her cruel husband in the revolution, thanks to the queen. She's barely shed a tear for him. Princess Imogen is a snake, but she's the queen's cousin. She likes the comforts such proximity affords her. And Lady Hendricks might have the capacity for such maliciousness, but she wouldn't be able to keep word of it to herself. I don't know the Russians, but the Blood court is infamous for poisonings."

"But why would they go to so much trouble when one of their princes is courting the queen?"

Malloryn smiled. "Why, indeed?"

Sir Gideon snapped his pocket watch open and then shut again. Five hours and no word. He trusted Malloryn's capabilities, but this was beginning to seem nothing short of torture.

The queen's head was bent over a book. She hadn't spoken a word to him since he'd arrived and made that statement. To force the issue meant breaking his word; and he was loath to do that, especially to her.

He flicked his thumbnail under the pocket watch's edge, popping it open again as he strolled toward the window.

"Good grief." The queen slapped the book flat in her lap. "Can you stop doing that?"

He stilled. "Doing what?"

"Checking your bloody pocket watch. If you wish to leave so dearly, then leave. I have guards at the door."

Sir Gideon straightened and popped the watch in his

pocket. "I'm not going anywhere. And I don't wish to leave. I was merely wondering what was taking Malloryn so long."

"Malloryn is no doubt stirring a hornet's nest," the queen replied. "It's what he does best."

"You almost sound as if you admire him."

She paused. "Few have been as loyal to me over the years. And while his methods may frustrate me at times, I do remember that."

"He frustrates me frequently," Sir Gideon admitted. "He wears all the arrogance of his class, though his loyalties cannot be questioned."

The queen set her book aside. "He may be a blue blood, and yet, it was his voice that recommended I choose you for the new council in the wake of the revolution."

Sir Gideon's eyebrows rose. He'd always wondered about that. He'd been head of the Humans First political party, the son of a minor house who'd forged a career in politics with his pacifist ways. Though he'd worked with the Duchess of Casavian to channel funds to the revolutionaries in the streets, he'd never expected to be named to the council.

"And now I owe him a favor," he grumbled. "I do wish you hadn't told me that."

"I trust him," she continued, "because while he is a managing busybody who cannot keep his nose out of anyone's business, he is also able to make decisions for the good of the realm, even when they do not necessarily benefit him. He makes suggestions he doesn't like, because he knows they are the right suggestions to make. And if you tell him I said that, then I will deny it with all my breath."

Sir Gideon shot her a faint smile. "Malloryn doesn't need compliments. He's already filled with his own sense of self-importance. And I would never repeat your confidences."

"I know." Her voice came soft. "I wouldn't take you into them if I didn't think you too were loyal."

The fire in the grate crackled in the ensuing silence.

"I would never betray you," he murmured.

"I know."

"And I would never—"

"I know," she snapped.

His lips thinned, but he hadn't won his way to the head of a political party by buckling at the slightest hint of stubbornness. "You don't know. For you didn't allow me to finish my sentence."

The queen stared at her hands. "You would never betray me. You are my most loyal subject. You believe in me. I've heard it all before, Gideon."

"I would never hurt you, is what I was going to say." He poured the pair of them a cordial. "Though I've never had cause to say that before."

Their eyes met as she accepted the cordial, and he could feel the faint tremor in her fingers as they brushed against his.

"I know," she whispered. "You would never hurt me."

It eased some of the tension within him.

Ever since he'd kissed her and she'd shoved him away, he'd felt as though a hot coal lingered in his stomach.

He had never set hands upon a woman who had not wanted his attentions, but this one most crucial time, he had misread her affections. And it curdled inside him, a secret shame that ate away at the honor at the very core of him.

"You should be resting," he told her. "Not sitting up and waiting for Malloryn to return."

"I barely had a sip of the poison, Sir Gideon. And you are not in any position to be telling me what I should or should not do."

Frustration got the better of him. "Forgive me for caring about my queen's health."

She shot him a startled look, then her eyes narrowed. "Your queen is going to survive the night, Sir Gideon. Lay your mind at rest. You won't be forced to deal with my replacement just yet."

"That wasn't what I meant, and you know it."

She set the empty glass aside and stood. "Do I?"

He wanted to tear out his hair.

It was one thing to watch her marry another. He'd always known it would come to this. She was the Queen of Britain, and he was merely a minor nobleman's son who'd risen to prominence through his political aspirations during the revolution. There had never been any hope for them.

But the foolish part of his heart that squeezed in his chest every time he saw her didn't care.

She was the woman he loved.

She was the woman he would always love, come what may.

Gideon threw back his cordial, then set the glass down with a hard crack. "I think we need to discuss what happened at Haver Hall."

"You kissed me," she blurted.

"And I apologized for that, most profusely. I had... misinterpreted your intentions and I was swept away in the moment. I should never have dared lay—"

A sharp rap came at the door, startling the pair of them.

The queen swished away from him, looking cool and regal. He hated how she could seemingly wipe the storm of emotion from her face in the blink of an eye—for all his skill with diplomacy, he could never quite manage it.

"Come in," she called.

Malloryn entered, stark in black. "Your Majesty." He bowed, then nodded toward Gideon.

"Any news?" Despite his frustration, Gideon got straight to the heart of the matter.

"My men have discovered the cook who laced the cordial and cakes with cyanide," Malloryn said grimly. "Unfortunately, he managed to take his own life before my Rogues could apprehend him, and we don't know why he made this attempt."

"A cook?"

Why would one of the palace servants bear such a grudge?

"I daresay it was a crime of opportunity, and the cook merely a playing piece in someone else's game," Malloryn replied. "My crime scene analyst assures me she's tested the amount of cyanide in your cordial and it's not enough to have killed you, though the ongoing complications may have made your health suffer dramatically. It was also placed in your cordial on a servant drone's tray, which anyone could have sipped from. The cook was no expert poisoner, which is a clue in itself—this was either a sloppy attempt made by a desperate man on behalf of someone else; an attempt to incapacitate you, rather than kill you; or merely a disgruntled servant taking matters into his own hands."

"Doubtful," Gideon murmured.

"I agree," Malloryn conceded.

"So we don't know who was behind all of this?" the queen said breathlessly.

"Not yet. But I will find them."

"Who would want to incapacitate her?" He didn't know why, but that option caught his attention. The prince consort had kept the queen plied with laudanum and wine, and while she kept herself severely restrained now, he couldn't help thinking of the listless way she'd once signed court documents.

"I don't know." Malloryn met his gaze. "Yet. If the queen's health declined, the council would be in control of the empire until a regent could be appointed. But the council would be the one to appoint a regent, and so I cannot see this as a power grab."

Alexandra turned toward the fireplace, holding her hands out to the fire as if she felt a sudden chill. "It could be a ploy to force my hand," she whispered. "If I were struck ill, then Britain would be at a disadvantage. And you were right. I have no heir. Someone might be pushing me to forge a marriage as swiftly as possible. Failing that, it might be an attempt to force me to name an heir."

A thought occurred. "Maybe you weren't meant to drink the cordial? Unless they were completely inept, the culprit must know you're surrounded by blue bloods who might be able to smell the cyanide. It's a noticeable scent. Perhaps it was a scare attempt?"

Malloryn's brows notched together. "I didn't think of that. I'll add those motives to the list."

The queen nodded, but she looked a little more fragile in the early dawn light streaming through the windows.

It was one thing to know someone had put poison in your cordial; quite another to be coolly discussing why.

He wanted to reach out to her and clap a hand upon her shoulder. To set her mind at ease, somehow, and remind her that she was not alone.

But he did not have that right.

"I'm going to set a rotation of my female Rogues at your side at all times," Malloryn told her. "Gemma and Lark are both blue bloods, and Ingrid is verwulfen. If someone makes another attempt, they should be able to prevent it."

"And in the meantime?" Alexandra asked.

"Continue as you were. Let's not let them think us cowed by this attempt. We want to draw them out and encourage them to make another attempt." Malloryn smiled. "Only this time, we'll be aware that it's coming."

CHAPTER 5

The Royal Exhibition began the next day.

Alexandra pasted a smile on her face and went about her daily business as though there was nothing out of the ordinary. She breakfasted on the terrace, finished her correspondence, and then met the Duchess of Casavian by the carriage at 11am.

Mina greeted her with a smile and clasped both of her hands. In private they may once have shared a hug, but she still hadn't quite forgiven her friend.

"Ready to open the exhibition?"

"The question remains: Are you?" Alexandra arched a brow. "You're rarely out of bed by this time of the day."

"Unfortunately, Madeleine doesn't quite seem to understand her parents' nocturnal habits," Mina sighed. "Her craving virus levels are so low the sun doesn't yet bother her, which means her parents must face the day at a rather appalling time."

It stole a laugh from her. "She's with her father?"

"He's taking her to the zoo." Mina snorted. "I can't wait to hear what adventures they have. The last time he took her out for the day, I came home to find him snoring in the library with a book over his face."

"I'm sure he'll have more fun than we shall," Alexandra grumbled. "My goddaughter is eminently more interesting than an exhibition on the *Advances of the Steam Age*."

"Now, now," Mina chided. "Who does *not* wish to see the latest design in dreadnoughts?"

Alexandra sent her friend a stern look.

"Besides," Mina cooed, "I do believe you're going to be the center of attention, my dear. There are at least three of your potential suitors in attendance."

"I shall carry my smelling salts in case the excitement of their company overwhelms me."

Alexandra gathered her skirts to climb into the carriage, then paused when she saw Malloryn appear like a blighted raven. She paused, insisting Mina go ahead of her.

"Ah, my Master of Shadows."

"My queen."

"Anything I should be aware of?" she asked as Malloryn handed her into the carriage.

"The papers are filled with talk of Lady Rachinger's latest findings about the craving virus," he replied, as he handed her a newspaper. "She presented her scientific paper yesterday at the Royal Academy, and a journalist caught wind of it."

"The life expectancies treatise that she presented to the council three months ago?"

"Yes. I've had more invitations to dine with our foreign emissaries than you have. They all want to know what it means."

Mina leaned forward from the carriage. "Of course, they do, Malloryn. Most blue bloods in England leapt at the chance to use Lady Rachinger's "cure" to stave off the ill effects of the Fade. Several other countries took note. Now, they're concerned that it's going to decrease their mortality."

Alexandra shook out the paper. She rather liked Sir Henry's serious, intelligent wife. Lady Honoria spent her days studying the effects of her findings on the craving cure, and her latest discovery was creating quite the stir.

Several years ago, she'd been experimenting with her husband's increasing CV levels when she'd realized that by drinking her vaccinated blood, his CV levels decreased to a manageable state. It had been quite the coup, until she'd recently revealed that along with the decrease in the virus's bloodthirsty hold, it also decreased a blue blood's strength, speed, and longevity.

Lady Rachinger had concluded that her husband might only live as long as she would.

"One cannot live forever," Alexandra murmured, then caught Malloryn's eye. "And no doubt it's a great relief to know you may not outlive your pretty young wife, after all."

The duke sighed. "My CV levels were never absurdly high to begin with, so I've not yet begun a regime of drinking the blood from the vaccinated."

"But you will?" She wasn't entirely certain of his answer. To see the Duke of Malloryn succumb to his feelings for his wife had been highly amusing—and unexpected. But his downfall was so recent. What would win? Love? Or power and the ability to live well beyond human years?

"I will," he replied with little aplomb. "I've spent far too many years without Adele in my life. And now I've had a taste of what it can be like, I would not wish to live without her. What is immortality but the chance to live a long, lonely life as you watch your wife, children, and grandchildren pass before your eyes? I would prefer to live one life in full."

The queen hid a smile. "How romantic, Malloryn. I would never have expected it of you."

"If it's any consolation, a year ago I would have agreed with you." He closed the carriage door. "A marriage for the sake of duty is all well and good, but when one finds affection, loyalty, and a true meeting of the minds, one can be free to be their best self."

"Ah, I see." She stilled. "This is supposed to be the part where you give me a hint as to where to settle my affections?"

Malloryn cocked his head. "I think your affections quite fixed, are they not?"

A shock of heat thrilled through her.

He couldn't know, could he?

The duke's smile widened as if she'd betrayed herself. "Give my regards to Prince Ivan. He did mention that he'd be awaiting you at the exhibition."

MALLORYN WAS CORRECT.

The prince lay in wait the second she cut the ribbon and pronounced the exhibition open to the viewing public—which, of course, meant the elite, or at least, it did for the first day.

Alexandra tried to enjoy herself.

The exhibitions were indeed intriguing. Inventors from across the globe had come to try their hand at the exhibition's prize, which she'd set herself. The Queen's Purse. And possibly patronage from the royal house. This might have been the inaugural exhibition of its type, but she hoped to continue the tradition. It had been the product of both her and Sir Gideon's imaginations, a scheme drummed up beneath gaslight as they played chess.

Blue bloods had ruled too much of Europe thus far.

She wanted the human members of her realm to have a chance to compete with them on an even scale, and where better than the mechanical arts?

It was also a chance to push the boundaries of technology and encourage the young scientists of the empire—as well as those from abroad. She wanted her empire to be considered a world leader, and in the wake of the upheaval of the revolution, this had seemed a perfect way to flaunt Britain's might.

"And which exhibitor has caught your interest?" the prince murmured as they strolled through the galleries, ahead of a pack of his cohorts.

She glanced around. "There are too many to name just one. Which exhibit interests you?" she asked politely, to see if his choices could give her some insight into his character.

He immediately brightened. "The Scandinavian kraken submersibles. Though my interest may have something to do with their latest designs and the way the patrol the Baltic Sea. There have been several encounters with Russian ships."

"Ah, so you seek further insights into their strengths and weaknesses."

He shrugged. "Our peoples prepare for the renewal of the Treaty of Stockholm this summer. The terms of the treaty were originally set one hundred years ago, and this is the first time we have had a chance to renegotiate them. It may be… an interesting time."

"The Scandinavians are allies of Britain," she reminded him. "They are our good friends."

"Then perhaps Russia needs to become your ally too? Perhaps we also could be your friends?"

"Perhaps. Is that why you're here, Prince Ivan? To further the interests of your people? Is it duty that drives your presence?" she teased.

"Duty that insisted I come, though I will concede to being pleasantly surprised." He smiled at her. "Duty has never seemed so enjoyable before."

Prince Ivan lifted a hand, capturing her cheek in his leather-clad palm.

Alexandra froze.

Not only was it the height of presumption and discourtesy, but she couldn't say a thing. Her body simply stiffened, the way it always had when her husband loomed over her.

She was shutting down like an automaton, her circuits awry, the noise turning into a fierce babble around her.

Prince Ivan's nostrils flared, as if sensing prey. He lowered his hand. "I have offended you."

Relief burst over her like a cascade, and suddenly sound rushed back into her ears. "Offended, no? Presumed, yes."

She stepped away, and he let his hand drop, a faint, perplexed indent between his brows.

"Pray excuse me," she said, turning to walk away before he could reply. She almost slammed into one of his companions—the Grand Duchess Xenia Nikolaevna—before staggering away from the voluptuous blonde with a stammered apology.

It was only when she was in the privacy of the hallway that she allowed herself to relax.

She was perspiring so badly, she felt as though she'd run all the way to Windsor and back.

Alexandra looked down at her clenched fists.

Prince Ivan had barely touched her.

He hadn't meant to offend her in any way, he had simply been attempting to… to court her. And she'd frozen like a deer sensing the hunter's rifle locking upon her.

"I hate you," she whispered to her long-dead husband. "And I will not allow you to haunt me now. I will forget you. I swear I will."

She was the queen. She would *not* run from her duty.

But she was wise enough to admit that this one time, she might need help to do so.

A KNOCK CAME AT THE DOOR OF ALEXANDRA'S ANTECHAMBERS.

"Come in," she called, a flutter of nerves assaulting her. Turning, she swiftly poured two glasses of cordial, almost knocking one of them over in her haste. Damn it. This entire plan had seemed a good idea at the time, but now the moment had arrived, she couldn't help feeling overwhelmed.

She was a woman. A queen. Married once, and then widowed. It wasn't as though she was some lily-livered virgin who'd never encountered a man.

Yes, whispered her conscience, *but this is different, and you know it is.*

Sir Gideon entered, his dark eyes finding hers instantly. He was such a tall, imposing figure with his broad shoulders and well-trimmed physique. At first, she'd found him a little intimidating, for he was prone to stern looks and rarely smiled. But she'd soon grown used to his well-measured voice and the gentle way he could steer an argument without even raising his tone.

He was the sort of man who was polite to all her servants, even when he didn't realize she was watching—and she had watched him often, from the secrecy of the chambers that had once riddled the Ivory Tower. She'd seen him placate a housemaid who'd spilled an entire bucket of mop water on his elegant shoes with a gentle smile that eased the girl's tears, and he'd been the first to wade into a carriage accident when it occurred right in front of him, working without care for his attire or even personal injury. When it became clear the lead horse would never draw a carriage again, he'd bought it and put it out to pasture.

Kindness. It had been such a rarity in her life that she'd found herself perplexed by it at first, until she realized that was just the sort of man he was.

"What's wrong?" he asked, noting the spilled cordial and the way she stared.

Suddenly, she couldn't do it. "Nothing. Nothing's wrong." Swishing toward the windows, she curled her fingers into a fist in her gloves. What a fool she'd been.

"Alexandra," he chided.

"I was just…. I was thinking of this entire bloody affair,"

she bit out. "There's barely a week left of the exhibition. And Malloryn will expect an answer, and I-I don't have one. I don't care for any of them."

Silence fell like a lash.

She spun around. "Say something."

Gideon lowered his eyes. "You don't have to choose a suitor this week. Malloryn can't force your hand. There is time, Alexandra."

Her name. On his lips.

Only here, in the privacy of her chambers.

She closed her eyes, lingering in the sound of her name. "If not now, then when? Nothing will change. Not this year. Not the next. I will always find some excuse."

"If you don't care to take a husband, then I will back you in the council meetings," he told her firmly.

"No." Alexandra shook her head. "You don't understand. Malloryn makes sense. I don't like it. I don't want to take a husband, but he is right. I didn't fight this entire bloody civil war just to risk instability because of my cursed feelings. I am queen. And I need to produce an heir for my country. But I... I don't know if I can."

Though Manderlay had kissed her, the only man who had ever bedded her had been her husband.

Gideon coughed into his hand. "Perhaps this is a conversation you should be having with your physician."

Alexandra swallowed the lump in her throat. She had stared down every blue blood in the Echelon. She could do this. "It doesn't stem from a physical inability. I need... help."

"Help? Of course, Alexandra. Anything that is within my power to give." Concern touched his voice, and she could sense him pausing behind her, always that bloody infernal foot of space between them.

Alexandra bowed her head, praying for strength. "I need for you to kiss me," she whispered.

And... nothing.

Nothing came. No answer. Not even a sucked in gasp of breath.

The ensuing silence lingered for so long, that a sudden spark cracking in the grate startled them both.

It broke her from her silence.

"Forget that I asked," she said, turning abruptly and sweeping toward the door.

Or, at least, that was her intention.

"Wait." Gideon reached out, his hand pressing against the wall, and she found herself trapped between the overwhelming press of his body and the warmth of the fireplace behind her. "I wasn't saying no. You caught me by surprise. I had assumed you were not.... That is.... You practically fled from me last time."

"It wasn't because of you," she admitted, and it galled that she must even confess to this. The words came in a rapid spill. "When you kissed me, I was fine. I... I wanted you to kiss me. But the moment you pressed me against the wall, all I could see was him. All I could feel was the hard press of his hands—"

She turned away, balling her fists.

"Alexandra." A whisper of fabric indicated he'd moved.

She could sense him behind her. Sense the heat of his body in a way she'd never felt from her coldblooded husband.

"I cannot marry if I can barely stand to be touched," she admitted, swallowing the lump in her throat. "I cannot produce an heir for the realm if the mere presence of a man in my bed makes me recoil. I can't— You're the only one whose kiss doesn't make me feel ill. If you taught me how to be kissed, how to be touched, perhaps I could stand it. Perhaps I could forget him. Perhaps I could endure another marriage."

"Turn around," he said.

"Must I?" For the truth was written large upon her face, and she didn't think she could control it, just this once.

Gentle fingers brushed against her spine, sending a shockwave of sensation through her. "Please."

Alexandra turned.

Gideon's dark eyes swam with sorrow. She could spend hours drowning in those eyes, swimming in the depths of the man who wore them.

If only….

"Why didn't you say something?" he whispered, the backs of his fingers brushing against her cheek.

"What woman wants to admit to such shortcomings?"

His expression hardened. "They are not *your* shortcomings. The fault for this lies entirely with your husband. I would kill him for you and set him on bloody fire, if he was still alive."

"I don't want that," she whispered back. "He is dead. He is gone. Rotting in the ground for all I care. I just want to forget him. I want to forget his face, his voice, his… touch. Make me forget, please."

Cupping her face in both hands, he tilted her lips toward his. Their eyes met, and she was reassured by the warmth and compassion she saw in his gaze.

"I shouldn't kiss you," he whispered, brushing his mouth across hers.

"Why not?" she breathed, wilting into the gentleness of his touch.

"Because it makes me want what I can't have," he admitted hoarsely.

And then he captured the gasp on her lips.

It stole her breath. Burned through her, as though sheer exhilaration raced through her veins. She felt like she was sixteen again, yearning for all the things she didn't quite understand, before the prince consort had stolen away that future by forcing her into marriage.

This. This was precisely what had happened the last time Gideon had kissed her.

She'd almost thought it had been a trick her mind played, but no, it was real. Alexandra leaned into the embrace with a soft moan, silently begging for more.

Each touch of his hands was gentle, and the soft, lazy trace of his tongue made her yearn for more. Alexandra pushed into the kiss, but he retreated, as if to say, if she wanted more, then *she* would have to be the one who took it.

Soft fingertips traced beguiling circles on her cheeks. It was a whisper of a touch—like nothing she'd ever felt before. It tempted her as nothing else could. She wanted those roughened palms on her skin, on her hips. Stubble grazed her chin, and she wanted to feel it rasping against her sensitive breasts.

"My queen," he whispered, drawing back for breath, his dark eyes ablaze with need.

She'd never tasted desire like this. "Don't stop."

"We have to."

She captured a fistful of his hair. "I make the rules. And I say no, we don't." But right at that moment, some sound began to intrude into her thoughts. She drew back, her brow creasing together. "Is that...?"

A repetitive knock on the door echoed through her chambers.

She swiftly turned away, putting several feet of distance between them. It wouldn't do to be caught in such a compromising situation, though a swift touch of her cheeks revealed the blazing heat of them. "Come in," she called, smoothing the wrinkles in her skirts.

The door opened, and one of the maids came in, laboring under the weight of a heavy tray. "My apologies, Your Majesty. You sent for tea?"

She had. In the hopes that she could take tea with Gideon before she broached such a sensitive subject. Goodness. She'd almost forgotten.

"Thank you, Clara," she said, gesturing to the smaller table by the fireplace. "You may set it down there, please."

Gideon stared out the window as the housemaid fiddled with the tea setting. She couldn't read the firm set of his shoulders, but she envied him the ability to hide his face. She was certain hers bore the stain of her recent activities.

The queen cleared her throat. "That will do, thank you, Clara."

She waited until the maid had curtsied and closed the door behind her, before turning back to Gideon. "Will you not look at me?"

He slowly turned around, clasping his hands in front of him. "It was not you I was trying to avoid."

"No?"

"No," he growled, tugging at his necktie. "You've left me quite undone."

A laugh escaped her as she began to gather his meaning.

And what a wonder that was—that she could find amusement in such a state of affairs, when she'd only ever seen a man's attentions as something to be endured. This situation with Gideon was completely confusing.

"Come here," she whispered. "Kiss me again. And this time, don't stop."

"But your tea will grow cold," he teased.

"Gideon," she growled.

He laughed and strode toward her. "As you wish, my queen."

CHAPTER 6

"Well?" the Duke of Malloryn asked as he and Gemma took tea.

Clara smoothed her skirts as she took her seat, shooting him a chastening look. "I thought I was placed within Her Majesty's household in order to prevent an assassination?"

"Yes, yes," he said, waving a hand. Clara Herbert was one of his best spies. A true chameleon with a nondescript face and manners, she could blend into almost any background. He'd recalled her and Herbert from Bath the second the queen was poisoned. "Let's not pretend that was the only reason."

"It is possible Her Majesty and Sir Gideon were having an intimate conversation when I entered."

"A conversation?"

Clara returned his glare with a steady gaze. "They were three feet apart, though I suspect they were closer before I entered. The queen was breathless, her skirts a little creased, and her lips reddened. There was no sign of her usual equilibrium and her gaze kept straying to Sir Gideon's back. He turned away from me the moment I entered, perhaps encumbered by something he couldn't quite hide. Either they were having a heated discussion, Your Grace, or they were embracing. And I suspect Sir Gideon enjoyed it."

Good grief. "You've been spending too much time with Gemma."

Gemma snorted, stirring her tea with a finger. "If she'd been spending too much time with me, she'd have been blunter. Sir Gideon had a cockstand on him the size of Africa, I'll wager."

Malloryn pinched the bridge of his nose. "Thank you for that image, Gemma."

"My pleasure, Malloryn."

He ignored her. Arguing with any of the Rogues, he'd discovered, was like trying to herd cats. "Thank you, Clara."

She curtsied, then dismissed herself.

Gemma set her teacup on its saucer. "Perhaps you should simply suggest the queen marry him, Malloryn. I daresay there's no need for these elaborate games. She seems quite fond of him, from what I've seen."

He peered down his nose at her. "Have you ever *tried* to make the queen do something you suggested? Headstrong does not quite cover it."

"Perhaps she is tired of being pushed and pulled in every which direction by the men who've tried to steal her power."

His eyes narrowed. "I have *never* tried to steal her power. I have only ever tried to protect her and the throne."

"Protect her? Or control her?"

His mouth gaped open.

Gemma shook her head, pushing to her feet. "I love you, Malloryn, but you grew up in a world where you were a male born into an aristocratic blue blood house, and hence had all the power in the realm. I understand why you fight for the oppressed, but you have never been one of them. You can see their struggles, but have never personally felt them. And the queen, for all her power, has.

"Perhaps you don't try to steal her power, but you

certainly try to control it. And while you may argue that you're the type of man who tries to control everything, when it comes to the queen, what makes you any different than any of the others?"

The heat blanched from his skin.

He was not—

He did not mean—

Gemma leaned down to kiss his cheek. "To truly serve your queen, perhaps you need to start listening to her and not presuming you know best."

Gemma's words stayed with him throughout the day, until Malloryn was almost pacing with frustration whilst Adele attended her toilette. They were due at the opera within the hour, but he could barely think of anything else.

"Do you think I am too controlling?" he asked.

Adele looked up from where she was rolling a stocking up her leg. In most instances, he'd have been focused on removing it right now, but not even she could distract him. "In what way? In an 'I am the Duke of Malloryn and I know best kind of way?' Or in an 'I am the Duke of Malloryn and I am trying to protect the people around me kind of way?'" She cocked her head on an angle. "Sometimes they both seem a little similar, if one is being honest."

Malloryn sank onto the bed and repeated what Gemma had said to him, feeling again the horror of shame. "I mean well—"

"I know," she said blandly.

"And I've only tried to...." To help. To steer.

Adele listened to him, her blue eyes unblinking, and then she sighed. "You have good intentions, my love, but sometimes intentions aren't good enough. Do you try to control the queen? Sometimes. Why do you think she always pushes back against you?"

To hear it from Gemma was bad enough, but Adele wasn't trying to even pull her punches.

"Sometimes, I think she walks into council chambers prepared to fight you before you even open your mouth," she continued. "If you think her headstrong, then perhaps you're to blame for creating such a drive within her."

He collapsed back on the bed, rubbing his hands over his eyes. "I'm tired of fighting with her. And the worst thing is, I wish she trusted me more, but perhaps you're right. Perhaps I'm to blame for nurturing that distrust. I've pushed her too hard in the past. And now, arranging this little coup, pushing her into marriage—"

A knee slid into the mattress on his right side, and then Adele crawled over him, seating herself in his lap. She captured his hands, dragging them from his face and holding them in her lap.

"What do I do?" he asked. "We're at a crucial juncture in rebuilding our nation. If I step back and grant her the freedom she clearly wishes, am I throwing her to the wolves? What if it all goes wrong? Somebody is already trying to kill her."

Adele kissed his palms, one after the other. "If the queen desires to rule without being challenged by her councilors, then perhaps you should grant her the leniency to do so. But firstly, I think you should apologize to her."

He scowled. "You know I hate that word."

Adele shot him a dazzling smile. "You might be surprised to see how far groveling will get you. It works with me, does it not?"

"I don't think the queen will appreciate it quite as much as you do."

"I should hope not. You are mine, after all." Adele leaned

forward, resting her weight on the palms of his hands. He curled them back against his chest.

A loud sigh escaped him. "Apologize. Very well."

"And soon," she pointed out.

CHAPTER 7

The clock on the mantel in her drawing room struck twelve.

The queen stared into the banked embers in her grate, clenching and unclenching her hands as she waited. What was she doing? What had she been thinking to even broach such a proposal with Gideon?

She pressed her fingers to her lips. If she concentrated she could still feel her lips tingling. That. That was why it had to be him.

A sharp rap sounded on the paneling of the wall, and she swiftly crossed to one of the tapestries and unlocked the hidden door.

A cloaked figure stepped through, towering over her. Then Gideon brushed the hood of his cloak back, revealing the stern, aquiline nose she adored so much and the rasp of the evening's growth of stubble on his chin. His dark hair was damp, as if he'd come directly from his bath, but he hadn't shaved.

"Are you going to let me in?" he asked, in his deep voice.

Alexandra realized she was staring and hastily stepped out of his way so he could shut the paneling behind him.

And then they were alone in the room together, with her proposition hanging in the air between them.

"What do you want of me?"

All her experience in the marital bed had been rough and rushed and driven purely by the interests of her husband. But she'd seen Mina glowing with happiness every time she looked at her husband, and from the saucy *on dits* Mina had shared, she'd managed to gather that the bedding was more than pleasant for her friend.

A part of her couldn't even fathom such a thing—but then she remembered the soft lushness of Gideon's kiss.

Pleasant, yes.

Far more than pleasant, if she was being honest.

"I don't know what I want," she admitted, straightening her shoulders. "My experiences have not been... kind. I can barely stand to be touched. That. That is what I want. To know if there is a part of me that can enjoy the experience. To no longer be afraid of being touched. And I'm not afraid. Not of you."

"Just how far do you intend for me to take this?" he asked softly.

Alexandra almost choked on her cordial. "I don't know."

He nodded slowly. Thoughtfully. Then began to slip his cloak off. "I see."

She considered the gossip she'd heard from Mina. "I do not think it would be wise to engage in lovemaking. I will not risk a child. I have heard, however, that there are ways...."

He dropped the cloak on the nearest chair and began to remove his gloves. "French letters, yes. Though I will be honest and admit they're not always successful."

A tremor of nerves ran through her, as he tossed his gloves carelessly on the chair behind him. "What are you doing?"

Gideon paused. Looked up.

And the world dropped away from her as she fell into those dark, dark eyes.

"Getting comfortable," he said, the heavy timbre of his voice dropping to depths she'd not even known he could reach.

There was something sensual about the way he said it. And then he moved to his coat. One button. Two. All the way down. Beneath it, he wore a charcoal gray wool waistcoat and a shirt and tie, but the way his fingers stroked over each button made it feel indecently intimate.

"Alexa?" he said, and she realized he'd repeated it twice.

Alexandra blinked. "Yes?"

"And tonight? What do you wish of me tonight?"

Good grief. This was happening. *Nothing*, she wanted to cry. *I was wrong, this is too much....*

But he slipped the coat from his shoulders and she forgot what she'd been going to say.

Gideon was unlike every other man of her acquaintance. Though Malloryn was taller, Gideon dwarfed him through the shoulders. His chest strained at his waistcoat, and as he slipped his hands in his pockets and stared back at her, the wool of his pants tightened over those powerful thighs.

Everything. I want everything.

"Do you like what you see?"

"Yes," she whispered.

"Where do you wish to start?"

"I don't know," she whispered, so the two halves of her conflicted conscience could meet in the middle.

"A kiss," he murmured.

"I've had a kiss."

"Oh, Alexa." For the first time tonight, he smiled. "That was barely a kiss before we were so rudely interrupted." Stepping closer, he paused barely two inches away from her, looking down. "Tonight we won't be interrupted. Are you sure you're ready for this?"

The scent of his cologne swirled through her. Gideon. This was Gideon. And something seemed to click in her mind. She knew this man. She'd spent years trying not to glance at the careful way his hands moved and the fine flex of his shoulders within his coat. She'd spent years with her fingers itching to sink through the dark strands of his hair, always cut too long. For the first time, she had permission to take what she wanted from him.

"Yes," she said, tipping her chin up firmly so she could look him in the eye. "Though you don't make the rules here. I do."

The faintest of smiles touched his mouth. "You like to be in control."

I need to be in control. But she didn't say it. She'd spent years as a pawn, both her body and mind manipulated by others. She would *never* submit again.

"What are your rules?"

"A kiss," she said. "Tonight. And I want to touch you." Daring herself, she reached out and brushed her fingertips across his waistcoat. "I want to see you."

"As you wish." Reaching out, he rested his fingertips under her chin and slowly lowered his mouth to hers. "A kiss, then."

The soft rasp of his lips across hers sent a shiver through her. Alexandra closed her eyes and leaned into the caress, savoring the sensation of it. Soft. Gentle. Ridiculously gentle. She wanted more, but the second she pushed into the embrace, he captured her wrists and leaned back.

"Oh, no." His eyes were alight with some sense of devilry she'd never seen him wear before. "That was merely another taste. You haven't earned your kiss yet."

"*Earned* it?"

Gideon stalked past her, pausing by the fireplace to take up the snifter of cordial she'd had poured and tossing it back. Giving her a challenging look, he tugged at the tie around his throat, and then slid it loose. The buttons at his throat gave, and then he began to work on the ones at his wrists.

"Come here," he said.

He eased back on the daybed, slinging one arm along the back of it.

"I thought I was the one giving the orders," she replied, though she was intrigued. This was a side to Gideon she'd never known existed.

Gentle, yes. But firm. Determined. He was the rock who never yielded. She should have guessed he'd take command in his own quiet manner.

"Not in here," Gideon replied, his voice roughening just a little. "You make the rules, but I give the orders."

Alexandra sipped the brandy that remained for her. A part of her liked the insolent way Gideon lounged against the chair, the way he tilted his face back to watch her, exposing his throat. She had never touched; only been touched. And her fingers itched to explore.

In the end, it was her decision, and her decision alone.

The silk of her skirts swished around her ankles as she slinked toward him. Tension betrayed itself in the tensing muscles of his thighs, and then slight creases that formed at the corners of his eyes, but he didn't move.

Barely even breathed.

Every step she took felt like she crossed a field strewn with explosives, until finally, finally, she stood before him.

"And now?" she whispered.

"Sit on my lap," he said.

Queens didn't perch on laps, she told him with a haughty arch of her brow.

"You're not my queen right now," he replied, "you're just a woman. And I'm just a man."

So be it. Sweeping her skirts out of the way, she perched herself gingerly on his thighs. Gideon's fingers took the glass from her and rolled the cordial back and forth, his eyes dipping to her neckline, but he made no move to touch her.

How utterly vexing.

"Are you going to make me beg at every step of the way?" she demanded.

"I don't intend to make you beg at all," he promised, capturing the fingers of one hand between his. "I'm the supplicant here, Alexandra. Not you."

"Then what—?" *What next?* It chafed her pride to be so at odds and ends here, uncertain of the next step and forced to rely upon his dictation.

Gideon seemed to understand.

"What do you want to do?" he asked, lifting her cordial to his lips and watching her.

The question flummoxed her.

"I want to kiss you again," she whispered, for she quite liked kissing. As long as it was him. "And not that foolishness of a kiss you just gave me."

He drained the glass and then set it aside. "Then kiss me. Do as you will."

Alexandra leaned down, cupping her palm against his cheek and the burr of prickles there. She captured his mouth, sighing into the taste of him. Gideon arched his throat, eating at her mouth with slow, lazy strokes.

Their tongues lashed together, and a small moan escaped her.

Goodness.

Something pressed against her hip, hard and indignant. It took her a moment to realize what it was, and she jerked back in surprise.

"I won't apologize for that," he said stiffly. "I'm only a man, Alexandra. I can't deny my attraction to you."

"It's not as though I've never encountered an erection before," she replied tartly, squirming a little. "Though I will admit, never quite of this… substance."

She glanced down curiously.

"Do you want to touch me? There?" he growled.

Alexandra looked up.

Why not?

Their gazes locked and she slid her hand between them, encouraged by the way he swallowed.

The brutish bulge within his breeches flexed as she worked his buttons. Every inch of him stilled, and a soft little sigh escaped him.

"Fuck," he whispered as her fingertips grazed the silky head of his erection.

She couldn't help herself. A giggle escaped her. "That's the first time I've ever heard you curse like that, Gideon. What terrible language."

"You'll hear more before we're through," he promised, shifting uncomfortably beneath her. "Like this," he growled roughly, curling her fingers around the length of him.

Alexandra looked down in shock.

She'd never realized how soft it would feel, the skin sliding loosely over its turgid length. Gideon moved her hand up and down, slowly pumping the slick steel of his engorgement.

Swirling her thumb over the satin-slick head of him, she indulged herself. Every twitch of her thumb drew a response from him. Soft sounds escaped him, and his teeth sank into his lower lip.

"Fuck." The word was torn from him.

More. She grew heady with her own power. "Is this the world-famous orator who brought the House of Lords to its knees?" she whispered in his ear. "Is that all you can say to me, Gideon?"

He captured the back of her head, his fingers sliding over a lock of her hair. "What do you want me to say?" he gasped. "That I've wanted you for years. That I've dreamed of you like this, in my arms. That I'm so fucking close to coming, I don't think… I can hold myself back." He threw his head back. "You undo me. You've always undone me."

Oh, she liked this.

Alexandra bit the soft, fleshy pad of his ear, and he bucked, a hot gush of liquid splashing over her hand. Gideon captured her hips, burying his face in her throat.

She held him for long moments, feeling flushed with success.

Dragging a shaking hand over his face, he shot her a glazed look, his breath still coming in soft pants. "That was not how this was meant to go. You've ruined all my best-laid plans."

Alexandra giggled, then glanced down at her hand.

"Here," he said, tearing his waistcoat off and using it to clean the pair of them up. He tossed it aside, then dragged his hand over his face again.

She barely had two seconds of warning.

One hot-eyed look, and then he hauled her into his arms, his mouth crashing down over hers.

A moment of shock assailed her, but she wasn't lost this time. She could still smell his cologne—the rich bay rum and spiced clove scent she always associated with Gideon.

He reached out, unbuttoning her gown. Callused fingers rasped against her skin, and she pushed into the touch. *Good grief.* She'd never known it could feel like this. Those hands on her skin were wreaking havoc, melting her from the inside out.

He barely had the top row of buttons undone, and then he was tugging impatiently at the cup of her corset. Alexandra gasped and arched her back, barely caring that her breast came free. A hint of heat filled her cheeks when she saw the look he gave her, and then his hot mouth locked over her breast, and Alexandra cried out. The sweet pull of his mouth felt as though it tugged directly between her thighs, and his tongue swirled slow circles around her nipple.

Too much.

Far too much.

She felt overwhelmed and undone in a way she'd never

felt before. The room spun, leaving her rocking against his thigh. Then his lips were rasping over her, teeth hard and firm, but also—

Teeth.

The exhilaration slid from her skin, as if she'd been dropped into the frigid Thames.

"Stop!" she cried.

The word echoed through the room as Gideon froze, lifting his mouth from her flesh. "Alexa?"

She tugged her corset back up, slipping her sleeve onto her shoulder again as she panted. What a mess she'd made of herself. Her skirts were all awry. She was still astride him, and the ache between her legs left her fidgety and frustrated with herself.

"Are you all right?" He reached for her hips, and she sent him a restraining look.

Gideon froze.

Alexandra pressed her face into her hands. Why could this not be easy? She'd been enjoying herself immensely. It had been perfect. So perfect. And then she'd ruined it the second his teeth grazed her nipple.

"I'm sorry."

She wanted to scream in frustration.

Soft fingers stroked her hair. "You have nothing to be sorry for, Alexa. I was the one who lost control. I should never have pushed you so far." His thumbs caressed her cheeks, and he slowly lowered her hands from her face. "You undo me in ways I am ashamed to admit."

Alexandra bit her lower lip. "We tried."

Gideon shook his head. "We're not done yet, my love. This was never going to be easy."

"But—"

"Here," he said, sliding his hand up her spine, and opening himself up to her. "Let me hold you. Listen to my heartbeat. It's still racing, and it's all for you."

Alexandra wilted over him, resting her cheek on his shoulder. His hand splayed up her spine, drifting in a soft, soothing motion. Up and down. Up and down. Inch by inch she relaxed.

Minutes dragged by. She lost track of time as she closed her eyes and threw herself into the pulsing rhythm of his heartbeat.

This was what she wanted. To be held, more than anything.

And until this moment she had not realized it.

"Don't let me go," she whispered.

"Never," he whispered back.

THAT NIGHT ALEXANDRA LAY ALONE IN HER BED, LISTENING TO the embers crack in the fireplace.

And she couldn't forget the warmth of his body and the firm press of his erection.

It was only in her imagination that she could be free, and she let her thoughts roam to areas she'd never dared consider before.

"What would you have me do?" whispered Gideon, and in her imaginings, he was on his knees before her.

"Strip," she replied.

Giving her an insolent look, he slipped his coat from his shoulders and let it fall to the floor. Never looking away from her hot-eyed gaze, he slowly began to work on his waistcoat and shirt, until he tugged the hem of the white linen from his trousers and revealed the heavy slab of his abdomen and chest.

A sprinkling of dark hair smattered his pectorals, but he wasn't finished. Sliding a hand down the trail of dark hair that dipped into his trousers, he popped several buttons and then paused.

Alexandra swallowed. "All of it."

His boots went flying. And then his trousers.

Finally he stood nude before her, every firm inch of him gleaming beneath the candlelight. He crossed to the bed toward her, his buttocks and his powerful thighs flexing.

"Take yourself in hand," she ordered.

Watching her the entire time, he skated his palm down his lean belly and firmly grasped his member. Despite the size of his hands, he couldn't entirely close his fingers around it.

The ache between her thighs increased.

Which was so confusing.

She'd never once thought a man's phallus to be worth anything more than pain. Though she'd learned to tolerate the bedding—with both the generous application of liniment and a glassful of poppy wine—it had never been anything less than a torment to be endured.

But this set off an entirely new sensation within her.

Alexandra brushed her fingers between her thighs, shivering a little. She felt exactly as she had when she'd been in his arms, his mouth on her skin. On the verge of something both overwhelming and terrifying.

She pictured Gideon kneeling on the bed and crawling up over her, those dark eyes focused intently. "What would my queen have me do?"

And as the queen stroked between her thighs, she thought of what she truly wanted from him.

"Love me," she whispered.

A smile touched his face. "I always have. And I always will."

CHAPTER 8

Fireworks lit the River Thames below them as the queen hosted a private party aboard a dirigible. *The Cardiff* was a pleasure-cruiser, confiscated from the Duke of Pendlebury during the Rising Sons revolt. Fitted out with gilded woodwork at every nook and cranny, its chandeliers glittered above the ballroom, shining light upon the polished wood of the floor.

Dancers swept in tidy circles as Alexandra smiled and flirted idly, swamped by potential suitors. It was just as she'd expected.

Flattery drifted unheeded past her ears. After dozens of years of meaningless compliments, she'd grown resistant to its effects.

Besides, it wasn't truly her that these foreign princes were trying to seduce. It was the queen. A figurehead only, a woman of power. The throne that they saw when they hinted at a potential alliance. Not Alexandra.

Never Alexandra.

She danced with a Hapsburg prince before finding herself in the arms of Prince Ivan once again.

This time she studied him.

It wasn't fair to compare him to her dead husband. He was neither similar in features nor in manners. And yet, she couldn't help feeling that suffocating sensation working its way up her throat the second he swept her onto the dance floor.

Too tall. Too broad of shoulder. Too powerful.

And overwhelming in his mannerisms.

Nothing was phrased as a question—though that could have been his grasp of the English language. And he drove her through the waltz like a master wielding a fractious horse.

Every now and then she caught a glimpse of one of the Grand Duchesses watching her from the sideline, staring sullenly over her wine. Light gleamed off the woman's gilt-colored hair, and her dress was cut low enough to display an impressive bosom.

She was everything Alexandra was not—except for being a queen.

"I do not think your countrywoman approves," Alexandra murmured, as the prince swept her beneath his arm.

Ivan glanced in the duchess's direction, then shrugged his shoulder. "Ignore her. Xenia thinks herself beyond her station. She is competitive in all matters."

"Is she competition?" Alexandra jested.

His jaw tightened in a way she didn't quite like. "No. Though she would wish to be."

Alexandra couldn't help shooting the other woman another glance. The hot-eyed look made sense now, and it made her a little uncomfortable.

"I think I would like some fresh air," she murmured, trying to disentangle herself the seconds the dying strains of the dance sounded.

"Of course." Ivan gallantly offered her his arm.

Alone, she'd meant.

But she pasted a smile on her face and allowed him to

escort her onto the foredeck. The second they arrived, she let his arm go.

"Wine?" he asked, thrusting the glass toward her.

It was not a suggestion, and to deny him would be to cause a scene. Alexandra accepted the glass, lifting it to her lips with a placating smile, but not drinking. "Thank you."

She often found she needed to say very little when he was around, as he filled the silence himself.

"These are interesting ships," he said, patting the edge of the rail. "In Russia, it is too cold to 'take the air' as you English do. And the helium in the dirigible envelopes freezes, which makes them dangerous during the winter months." He looked down at the lights glittering across London. "But this is an excellent pastime. My people would enjoy this."

He continued praising the airship's abilities and decorations.

And then he praised her city, though he wished he'd been able to see the Ivory Tower before it fell—a marvel of the modern age.

And then he began to praise her beauty. And her kindness. And her benevolence.

Alexandra's eyes began to glaze over.

Help arrived in the form of Sir Gideon.

"Ah, there you are," he said, offering her a glass of watered cordial and making it seem as though she'd requested the drink long ago. "I meant to bring it to you earlier, before being waylaid by Malloryn."

"You care not for wine?" Prince Ivan murmured, his hawkish eyes watching every move she made.

Alexandra sipped her cordial. "It disagrees with me."

She'd spent enough years drifting in a fogged stupor—the only means she had of dealing with her husband's cruelty. Too much wine. Too much milk of poppy. It had been an escape for her, but the effects were frightening. Once she'd killed him, she'd spent six months trying to ease its hold on her.

She never wanted to return to those days.

The sweats, the hallucinations, and worse, the sheer driving *need* to let it wash over her again. The desire for obliteration.

She did not even dare take a sip of milk of poppy these days, for fear she would crave it again.

"You did not say," he said.

Gideon coughed into his hand. "The queen is the epitome of politeness. I daresay she did not wish to be rude."

Prince Ivan looked between them. "But what do you drink if you do not drink wine?"

"Many things, Your Highness. Have you heard of the restorative effects of cordials?" Gideon began, and he somehow genuinely managed to sound as though this was the most scintillating conversation he'd ever had.

A woman exited the ballroom, glittering like a star beneath the gaslight in her drapings of gold. Jewelry glittered at every finger, and earrings dripped from her ears. There was even a slim coronet on her head.

"Cousin Imogen," Alexandra called, catching a glimpse of her old rival.

Princess Imogen stiffened before gracing her with a smile. "Your Majesty."

"Have you met Prince Ivan? Your Highness, this is my cousin, Her Royal Highness, Princess Imogen of York."

It was unkind of her, truly it was, but she knew her cursed cousin wouldn't be able to resist a chance to ingratiate herself.

The woman was a good ten years older than she and resented the fact her mother, Princess Amelia, had not been born a man, as she was the eldest of her siblings and hence could have been granted the crown instead. It had taken Alexandra many years to realize why her cousin resented her, though the woman was harmless enough.

"Your Highness," Princess Imogen breathed, glancing up from beneath her lashes coquettishly as the prince lifted her hand to his lips.

His gaze strayed directly to her chest. Clearly he was a man of simple tastes.

Alexandra glanced at Gideon, and he smiled faintly in return, as if they were both thinking the same thing.

"I came to fetch you," he said. "Malloryn wishes to speak to you before the speeches."

"He does?"

"He does," Gideon said, staring her baldly in the eye.

Oh. "If you will excuse me, Your Highness," Alexandra said to the prince. "Duty calls. I'm sure my cousin will be a fine replacement."

Prince Ivan seemed to realize his prey was vanishing. "And yet, my heart grows empty. No woman could replace you within it. Will you save me a dance?"

"Of course." Inwardly, she sighed.

But at least she would have a moment away from him. They made their goodbyes and she practically fled.

"They make a handsome couple," Gideon murmured as the pair of them ducked away.

"Yes. They suit each other." She gathered her skirts. "The prince adores speaking of himself, and my cousin enjoys her own self-importance. Now, does Malloryn truly wish to see me?"

"No. I lied."

"How shocking, Gideon. I thought you were a paragon of honesty."

"I was afraid my queen was going to launch herself over the rail in the pursuit of escape. I risked my honor to save her life."

"You're dreadful." But she laughed. "Thank you. Now, perhaps I can reward you with a dance?"

"Perhaps I should take all of them, so you won't be

encumbered by that enormous lout."

Alexandra offered him a secret smile from across the deck. "Now, now, Gideon. If I granted you all of my dances, people would whisper that I was intending to court *you*."

His dark eyes met hers, and he almost seemed to want to say something.

But then the door opened, light and laughter spilling out, and she could not ask.

∼

THREE MORNINGS LATER, ALEXANDRA FOUND HERSELF ONCE more at bay.

She'd just mounted the handsome gray mare she preferred when Prince Ivan appeared out of nowhere.

"Your Majesty. What luck. I was going for a ride this morning, too." He snapped his fingers, and one of the grooms led a fractious black stallion out, fully tacked.

"What luck indeed," she replied dryly.

Was Malloryn behind this?

She couldn't imagine the duke would care to deal with this infuriating blue blood—and Ivan wasn't the sort to respond to Malloryn's bit well—but who knew? Someone was clearly feeding him information as to her common habits.

Not deigning to wait for him, she clicked her mare into a trot and rode out into the streets that would lead to Hyde Park. In the foggy morning, she could almost feel alone, ignoring the pair of guards who trailed her and the prince who spurred his horse after her.

She rode for almost an hour before she let her horse drop into a stroll, dropping its head to nuzzle at a grassy verge.

"You ride well, my queen," Prince Ivan called, easing to her side.

"Thank you."

"I have been meaning to speak to you alone." Prince Ivan

presented her with a small box. "I have a gift. A token," he said, "of my affection."

Affection. *Good grief.* She barely knew him, though she had to admit he was playing his role well. "Thank you, Your Highness. You are most kind."

She opened the velvet box.

A golden scarab brooch lay cushioned within it, to be tethered at her breast with a pin. She held it up, winding the small clockwork cog at the side of its body. Instantly, its wings began to flutter and it crawled over her fingers. "How lovely. My dearest friend, the Duchess of Casavian, has one just like this, though hers is a spider."

"They tell me they're all the rage in London," he replied.

She'd never seen them, but then, she was sometimes kept at a distance from the rest of the world. It was possible.

Alexandra pinned the little brooch to her lapel, admiring how well the gold flickered in the early dawn light. "Thank you. It's lovely."

"A beautiful gift, for a beautiful queen."

Yes, well. She forced a smile, and then decided she may as well make conversation. She couldn't say "thank you" again. "Are you enjoying London?"

"Very much so." He immediately brightened. "There is much to do here, and I would enjoy prolonging the experience."

"You are one of Catherine's favorite great-grandchildren, though," she protested. "Surely your great-grandmother would desire your presence at court."

"She has not roused for many years. I believe this summer may well be her last." He shrugged and then gave her a steady look. "It may not be wise to be a grandchild in the court when she passes."

Catherine's eldest, whom she'd named heir, had been murdered, and now the rest of them scrambled for position.

"Ah," she said. "Perhaps a summer in the south, then?"

"Perhaps." His horse tossed its head, and he looked her in the eye. "Though I have hopes I may be spending it here."

A little presumptuous. She smiled. "Not as warm and sunny as the Mediterranean, though London comes alive during the summer. You would enjoy it."

"May I ask…? Sir Gideon is a friend, is he not?"

Alexandra froze. "Yes. A dear friend. He is one of the councilors that rule the city. The Duke of Malloryn is another. You have met Malloryn, yes?"

Prince Ivan's eyes hooded. "Yes, I have met the duke." And clearly not enjoyed the encounter.

Silence fell.

She could sense him gathering himself to ask another question, and nudged her heels against her horse's flanks. "Time to return, I think. There is to be breakfast on the lawn, and then I believe we are to play croquet. Malloryn will be there. I shall introduce you again—"

"And Sir Gideon?" This time he looked at her boldly.

Alexandra wheeled her mare. "I do believe so, yes."

CHAPTER 9

The next morning, the queen fled her suitors and found a quiet patch of lawn in the gardens.

Her solitude was not granted for long. A child's laughter echoed through the air, and then Mina came into sight with little Madeleine, holding a kite in her hand.

The second the little girl saw her, her face lit up and she ran to grant Alexandra a hug. "Aunt Alexandra."

The queen ruffled her hair, bending low to kiss her forehead. "My little rabbit. If you keep dashing about like that, you're going to trip and stain your pinafore."

Maddie smiled. "I never trip!"

Alexandra's smile faded as she looked up at her friend. "I see you're using my goddaughter against me."

"Nonsense," Mina replied. "It's a lovely day, and as your dearest friend, I've long been granted the run of the grounds here at Kensington. It was mere happenstance that we came across you."

"I've only just forgiven you," she replied tartly.

Mina clasped her hands in the kite's strings. "Excellent. I thought you were still avoiding me."

Alexandra turned away. "You presume too much."

"Always." Turning into the wind, her friend eased the kite out several lengths, then caught the string when it suddenly soared. "Here, Maddie-love. Make sure you stay away from the trees. I absolutely refuse to be climbing one today."

"Yes, Mama." Madeleine beamed at the pair of them as she accepted the string. The kite almost hauled her off her feet, but she used her blue blood strength to rein it in. Any normal child would have most likely fallen flat on their face.

"She looks like she's grown three inches," Alexandra murmured, as the little girl dashed across the grass, her kite pinwheeling through the sky.

Mina's smile slipped. "We've managed to find a formula that sustains her. Malloryn suggested it, actually. One of his Rogues discovered a protein solution that a blue blood can survive upon without being forced to drink blood."

The little girl had been born with the craving virus, but refused to drink blood. Alexandra couldn't say she blamed her, though poor Maddie had been sickly for most of her first year and cried incessantly until her parents realized she needed more than a wet nurse.

It was becoming a common affliction as more and more children were being born to blue blood parents—or to be more particular, blue blood mothers. Once upon a time, the Echelon had insisted only males be offered the rites that infected them with the craving, but with more and more women succumbing to the virus, they'd had to deal with this new problem that had arisen.

"It's a relief, I must admit." Mina fell into step beside her, and for once, her cool reserve faded. "There's nothing worse than not knowing how to help your child." Her face suddenly blanched. "I'm so sorry, Alexa. That was inconsiderate."

Alexandra turned away. "You didn't mean it."

"I know. But I shouldn't have mentioned it."

She watched little Madeleine curtsy to one of the gardeners. Maddie had her mother's auburn curls and dark eyes, but her smile was pure mischief, just like her father's.

A familiar pang of longing swept through her.

Edward would have been almost seven by now. She'd barely had a chance to see him before they'd taken him away, but he'd worn a wealth of thick dark hair—just like hers—and though his eyes had been forever closed, his little bow mouth had been all hers too. There'd been none of his father in him.

A hand reached for hers, and Alexandra swallowed as Mina squeezed. "He was a beautiful little boy."

"He was," she whispered. It never became easier to speak of it, but doing so kept the memory alive. "I miss him so much. He would have loved to play in these gardens."

"You should have a plaque erected here."

Alexandra released a slow breath. "Do you think so?"

"Beneath those trees," her friend replied, pointing to a shady corner. "And you can sit there when you want to visit with him. I can come with you, and Maddie can bring her kite."

She nodded briefly. "Thank you. That's a lovely idea. I'll talk to the head gardener."

They strolled along the path, both lost in silence. Sometimes she hated how her loss caused so many silences. Only Mina would dare speak of it with her, and she couldn't tell her dearest friend how much that meant to her.

Instantly, she forgave her for the vote against her interests.

"Are you growing weary of balls yet?" Mina asked.

"I'm growing weary of pretending to smile at some ill-conceived attempt at humor."

A laugh escaped the duchess. "Then don't. They're here to woo you. Not you them."

"I'm trying not to insult a foreign prince," she replied dryly. "England has enough enemies within, thank you very much."

"And have you any preferences?" her friend asked.

"Does it matter? My preference would be to remain unmarried, but my wishes are rarely taken into consideration. I think it more fitting for the council to tell me which of their candidates would be preferred, since they are running my kingdom for me at the moment."

Mina arched a brow.

Fine. She was still vexed.

"I don't believe the council as a whole has a preference, though I tend to agree with Malloryn's choice this one time," Mina replied.

"You *what*?" Alexandra stopped in her tracks. "Since when do you agree with Malloryn?"

"I always agree with Malloryn when he makes sense."

"Who? Who is it?"

"Oh, no." Mina shook her head. "If I mention a name, then I may inadvertently circumvent the entire process. You *are* stubborn, my dear."

"And *you* are a terrible friend." Alexandra strode ahead through the garden. "Plotting with Malloryn behind my back…. What does your husband think of that?"

"My husband merely rolls his eyes and tells the pair of us to leave you alone."

"Hmph. Barrons is an exceptional man with excellent sense."

A scalded sound echoed in Mina's throat. "Please don't tell him that. I'll never hear the end of it."

"I should throw a parade just for him."

"If you even think about it," Mina warned, "then I'll tell Malloryn you don't have enough suitors to contend with."

Alexandra slapped her with the fan that dangled from her wrist. "Truce."

"Truce." Mina caught her arm. "What a clever little brooch. It looks like my spider."

"Thank you." Alexandra turned her shoulder toward her friend. "It was a gift from Prince Ivan."

"Do you favor him?"

Alexandra strolled across the grass, picking her way through her words. "He has an excellent bloodline. Strong ties to the tsarina."

"Good teeth and a hearty constitution?" Mina murmured wryly. "You're not choosing a horse to race at Newmarket. Has he been kind to you?"

"He is brusque, and his interest quite clear." She sighed. "No, I do not favor him. I tolerate him because I must. Though perhaps he's been the most forthright of all my suitors. The Duke of Alba's brother can barely understand a word I say."

"Don't marry the prince," Mina said dismissively.

"Why not?"

"You don't care for him," Mina replied. "Choose someone you do care for."

"I don't have the luxury of insisting upon someone I care for," she replied curtly.

"If not love, then at least insist upon friendship," Mina chided. "I want to be happy for you. I want to see a smile on your face."

Alexandra sighed. "And I want a country that settles into a boring state of nonchalance, a council that doesn't try to impede me at every step, and an end to being shot at or poisoned."

"No word on the person behind the scheme?"

"Malloryn is still turning over rocks. You don't think the cook did it either?"

"I would like to be that naïve," Mina said shortly. "But if Malloryn thinks there's more to it, then I daresay he's right. He's no fool."

"Mama!"

They both looked to the right, where Maddie stood

forlornly beneath a pair of ash trees, her red kite hovering in the branches.

Mina sighed. "I swear if I told her to jump in the pond, it's the only time she wouldn't do it."

"I hope you have your climbing shoes on," Alexandra replied with no small amount of enjoyment.

"Do try not to enjoy this too much," Mina growled, hauling swathes of her skirt out of the way as she strode toward the tree.

"Oh, no," she called. "I'm going to enjoy every moment of it. It's the least you deserve."

"What do you think of this?" Alexandra murmured.

Malloryn clasped his hands behind his back. He seemed distracted, and she had to snap her fingers to capture his attention. Those stormy gray eyes blinked into focus. "Pardon?"

Alexandra straightened from the plans her architect had been drawing of Buckingham Palace. Her great-great grandmother, Queen Charlotte I, had completed its construction in 1836, but Alexandra's husband had always despised the place and preferred to create his own legacy. He'd persuaded her father, King Michael I, to begin renovations of the Banqueting House that remained from the Palace of Whitehall fires, down by the Thames.

After he'd overthrown her father and forced her into marriage, he'd insisted upon completing those renovations, though the project had expanded beyond thinking. It became known as the Ivory Tower, a shining beacon of purity that was supposed to rule over London forever. If there was one thing she could thank Lord Balfour for, it was destroying her husband's cursed monument.

And yet, such destruction now left her with no particular

residence to call her own. Windsor was too far from London. Kensington too small for her entire court. Her people needed to see her. They needed to be reminded that she was their queen and that all her husband's monuments were nothing more than ash and dust, just as he was.

And Buckingham suited her purposes. Or at least, it would.

"Are you ignoring me, Malloryn? Am I boring you?" she demanded.

"No," he replied sharply, then pinched the bridge of his nose. "My apologies. I was... thinking."

"Thinking." Alexandra straightened. "Do you possibly suppose you can think a little more on what I've been saying, and not on whatever is plaguing you?"

Malloryn stared at her.

Alexandra stared back. He was not behaving at all like himself. "Well?"

"There is something I must do first," he muttered.

And then, to her shock, he knelt at her feet.

"What are you doing?"

"Apologizing," he said. "It has been brought to my attention that I... I may push you too hard and try to manage you, when it should be the other way around. And I wanted you to know that I do not see myself as anything other than your servant. I am loyal, my queen. Even when I am... managing matters. I only have your best interests at heart." His voice roughened. "And if you wished for me to retire as your Master of Shadows, then I would do so."

Alexandra's mouth fell open.

Of all the things she'd never expected to hear....

"Good grief," she said. "Is this your wife's doing?"

His face twisted. "My wife did mention something about it, yes. Though it was Miss Townsend who first broached the subject." He looked up. "I was pushing you to marry, and I was wrong. You should be free to make your own choices."

"I *am* free to make my own choices." Alexandra swished around the table, heading for the decanter on the sideboard. She splashed a mouthful of cordial into a glass and then sipped at it. "Are you trying to tell me that you don't think I should marry?"

"Of course I think you should marry," he said, resting his hands on one thigh.

She arched a brow.

"I won't lie. It's exactly what I think you should do. But I went about it the wrong way. I conferred with several members of the council and maneuvered you into that vote. I knew which way it would go, and I deliberately backed you into a corner. I should have spoken to you about it, and only you. And then I should have trusted you to make the right decision." His face grew hard. "I've lost your trust."

"Stand up," she said firmly, because while a part of her did enjoy the sight of him on one knee, it also unnerved her a little. Malloryn was the weapon she always had at her back. And while that weapon sometimes rubbed her the wrong way, she slept better at night knowing he was out there, protecting her. "If I didn't trust you, Malloryn, I would have had you locked in a cell long ago. You're too dangerous and you know too much for you to go free, but I have always known that you reserve those instincts for those who remain enemies of the empire. And yes, you overstep yourself at times. And yes, you're a little managing"—she looked back down at her maps—"but sometimes, I may privately admit to myself that you are right, when I am wrong. I need you at my side to remind me in those moments. Too many others do not, and as my father always said, a wise ruler listens to even those who speak against her."

"And then does whatever the bloody hell one desires anyway," he said by rote as he stood.

It earned a smile from her. "He did say that, yes."

Malloryn leaned against the table, crossing his arms over

his chest. "He would have been proud of you, did you know?"

She stirred her fingers across the plans. "I like to think so."

Silence fell.

She could see thoughts racing through his eyes, as he clearly began to restore his equilibrium. And her first thought was that *that would not do*, but would she then be guilty of the precise thing he'd just apologized for?

"I will accept your apology," she said slowly. "And I am sure we will be arguing over the council table within a few months as if this conversation never happened. But you were right. I do not like the way you maneuvered my back to the wall. If you feel something needs to be done for the good of the empire, then come to me. I promise I will listen. And I promise I will think about a resolution. But your wife and friend are also right: I cannot continue like this. I need to know that I can trust you."

His focus seemed to have shifted again. He cocked his head and glanced to the side, frowning.

She wanted to slam her fist on that table. "Malloryn!"

Instead, he held a hand up. "What is that noise?"

"What noise?"

Crossing the room, he stalked along the bookshelves, narrowing in on the shawl she'd been wearing. Squatting down in front of the chair it hung on, he flipped it out, revealing a glimmer of gold.

Clinging to her shawl, the little scarab whirred its wings. What on earth was it doing? She hadn't wound it since this morning, and its functions had ceased several hours ago.

"Oh, that," she said, with some relief. "It's my brooch. Prince Ivan gave it to me. It flutters its wings and crawls across my bodice."

"Does it usually make that high-pitched whining noise?"

Alexandra rolled the plans up, frowning at it. "What whining noise?"

Malloryn flourished, and a knife suddenly appeared. He eased it under the scarab, and the little device crawled onto the blade. Beneath its carapace, it appeared to be glowing. Little lines of light showed where its seams met.

"No, it doesn't." She crept closer, but he held up a hand to keep her at bay.

"Something about this doesn't sit right with me."

"It's a brooch, Malloryn. They're all the rage in London, Prince Ivan said."

"London?" He looked up sharply. "How would he know that? He only arrived a week ago."

Alexandra backed away swiftly.

"It's too small," Malloryn said, almost to himself. He eased the tip of his knife under the carapace of the scarab, and the whining became audible to her ears as the scarab brooch began to thrash wildly. "There cannot be explosives within it."

"It's just a brooch. You're—"

A high-pitched scream echoed behind her.

Both of them spun toward the open windows.

"What was that?" she demanded.

Malloryn strode toward the window as a hawk-like shape circled past. "It appears to be some kind of gyrfalcon."

"A gyrfalcon?" Circling Kensington Palace?

He leaned out and closed the windows, then turned back to her. "I'm going to take the brooch down to Ava and see what she thinks. I'll send Gemma and Dmitri in to sit with you."

"You're starting to make me nervous, Malloryn."

"I'm just being careful."

Over his shoulder, a shadow began to grow larger through the glass. "Malloryn," she said, her gaze locking on the blur of movement.

He spun around.

Glass shattered as the gyrfalcon drove through it.

Alexandra screamed and thrust a hand up to protect herself, but the creature swept past her. Bronze wings flashed in the light, and she caught a glimpse of clockwork cogs whirring. Not a bird. A device.

With a high-pitched scream, the mechanical bird swooped directly toward Malloryn. He threw the scarab across the room, and the hawk immediately tried to bank, its head turning to track the scarab. It slammed into the wall behind Malloryn and exploded.

Alexandra threw up both arms.

A weight drove into her midriff—Malloryn, she thought—and she slammed into the floor as rubble pelted the pair of them. Heat rolled over her, the wind of its passage whipping her hair free from its neat chignon.

And then the warmth and sound died down, leaving her panting on the floor, listening to the crackle of fire.

"Are you all right?" Malloryn demanded, hauling her to her feet. Flames licked up the far wall, and half her books were on fire.

"My library," she whispered.

Another bird screeched in the distance.

Both of them looked to the row of windows.

"There's another one," he said breathlessly, yanking her toward the door.

Only there was no door. No door, no wall, no means to cross the gaping crevice in the floor. They were both trapped in the half of the room that lay untouched, and she turned her head slowly, finding the little scarab brooch fluttering its way across the floor behind her.

Malloryn's heel came down upon it with a crunch. "It's a tracking beacon."

Another piercing cry echoed through the windows.

"Come on!" he shouted, hauling her toward the enormous chasm in the floor.

"Malloryn!" she screamed.

Sweeping her up in his arms, he sprinted toward the gap and launched the pair of them over it. Guards ran toward them, and she saw a flash of startled faces before Malloryn landed with a jarring thud.

Alexandra spilled from his arms as they tumbled head over heel across the Aubusson carpets. Behind them, another loud, roaring explosion shook the building. The chandelier above her shivered, and several paintings fell from the walls as one of the guards slid to her side and threw himself over her.

"Your Majesty!"

"What happened?"

And Malloryn: "Secure the building. They're flying explosive devices. I believe I've destroyed the beacon summoning them, but we cannot be sure. Shoot down anything that flies toward the palace."

She turned to stare toward her favorite room. Flames licked up the doorframe, though half the wall was rubble. The rest of the room was gone. Simply gone.

"Are you all right?" asked the man who'd been shielding her.

She looked up into pale blue eyes. It was one of Malloryn's men. Byrnes, she thought. "I think so."

The words sounded distant.

"Take the queen to her chambers and set a rotating guard on the door." Malloryn pushed to his feet, his face stained with soot. "I think I'm going to want to have a word with Prince Ivan."

CHAPTER 10

Malloryn found the prince playing some form of backgammon in a parlor with several of his compatriots, though the rules seemed a trifle different.

"Your Highness," he greeted, with a faint tilt of the head. "May I have a word."

"You may have several, as I know you like to talk, Malloryn," Ivan announced, which earned a laugh from his friends. Though they'd talked but rarely, he swiftly realized Ivan saw him as some sort of threat.

"Alone."

The prince's smile vanished, and he flicked his fingers. The trio of his comrades disappeared, and the prince gestured to the chair opposite him.

"Care for a game?" Ivan asked.

"It seems familiar."

"*Nardy*," the prince replied with a shrug. He swiftly explained the rules, then dumped the dice in Malloryn's hand. "What do you wish to speak about?"

"Where were you an hour ago?" Malloryn rolled the die.

The prince lifted a cup of some foul-smelling spirits to his mouth. "I do not have to answer that."

"You don't." Malloryn considered his first move. "But you should. Someone tried to kill the queen earlier. I'm interested in your whereabouts."

"I was attending the Grand Duchess Xenia Nikolaevna in her personal suite." Prince Ivan's eyes glittered dangerously. "And be very careful what you're accusing me of. I may be your ruling prince one day."

Doubtful.

Especially if such attendance upon the duchess meant what Malloryn thought it meant.

"I'm accusing you of nothing." He tossed the dice and made a move. "I'm merely curious. Especially considering the brooch that you gave the queen was a tracking beacon for the devices used to target her."

Ivan choked on his mouthful. *"What?"*

Interesting.

He didn't seem to be overly concerned with an assassination attempt upon the queen, but the idea of having his name cast in the mud *did* bother him.

"Someone tried to kill her, and the only clue I have is the gift *you* gave her." Though he'd never expected Ivan to be behind this—only a fool would link himself so blatantly to a crime—it never hurt to make a suspect think they could be found guilty.

"I had nothing to do with that brooch! An Englishwoman suggested it to me! She said there was a jeweler in the city who created such devices and the queen would like it, for her friend has one. She said if I wished to give queen a gift beyond repair, then I should buy from him!"

A gift beyond compare?

Malloryn stilled. "Someone suggested you give the queen the brooch? Who?"

Ivan shot him a bewildered look. "She was one of the court ladies. A blonde with big—" He made a cupping gesture with his hands in front of his chest. "I do not remember her name. They all sound strange to me. And they all look the same. You breed pale, insipid women in this country."

"Who was the jeweler?"

"I don't know. In the city. My friend, Danil, he takes me there. He may remember the address. I gave it little thought. It was small and dirty. Not the sort of place I expected to find something for a queen, but the brooch, the brooch was magnificent, yes?"

It certainly was.

Malloryn pushed to his feet. "Which one is Danil?"

∽

THE URGE TO SEND FOR WINE—OR WORSE—GNAWED AT Alexandra as she made her way through the day.

One more day, she whispered to herself. *One more day without milk of poppy or wine. You are strong enough. You do not need it.*

The same cursed mantra she repeated to herself daily.

Speaking of Edward with Mina this morning had felt both somehow cathartic and also left a hollow, gaping wound within her.

But there was never a day she forgot him. Never a moment where she wouldn't see something and think, "oh, he would have loved those little toy soldiers" or "he would have been terribly bored at this banquet."

He filled her life, even seven years after his loss. And those memories were the brightest weapons against her ongoing fight to restrain herself from succumbing to a fugue. She lost those thoughts, those memories, when she was dull with poppy. He deserved better than a mother who floated through her life without emotion.

It didn't make it any easier.

She sat through several meetings and endured a formal

dinner with the council as they made plans to deal with the Scandinavian summit that was due to occur in May.

"You've been quiet," Gideon murmured as he lounged in the chair at her side. "You've recovered from yesterday's ordeal?"

"Too much on my mind. The past. The future." She sighed. "Mechanical birds plummeting out of the sky toward me."

"My queen worries too much."

"Don't we all?" She tried to make light of it.

He surveyed the council. "Perhaps, for once, we should enjoy what we have? One night where duty and obligation does not weigh heavily upon us. I am sure your subjects would not begrudge you one night."

"It is not my subjects who would begrudge it."

He met her gaze. "You hold yourself to high standards, I know. But you should be a little kinder upon yourself."

Alexandra sighed. "How many of my people suffered whilst I was forced to play my role beneath the prince consort's nose? How many of my people died because I dared not defy him too often?"

"Were you in control of the empire at that time?"

She scowled. "I was queen."

Gideon shook his head. "You were upon the throne, surrounded by an entire court of bloodthirsty predators. Your husband brooked little refusal to go along with his whims. I saw the way you would look at him when you dared to defy him. I saw your tremble, even as you held your head high and refused to look away. And I knew that defiance would cost you. We all knew it. Do you think I do not judge myself culpable for not doing something more to prevent such cruelties?"

"He would have killed you had you spoken out," she pointed out.

"I know. But perhaps one voice rising in defiance would

have allowed others the same bravery." Gideon stared into the distance. "I often wonder if my silence cost you and the realm far more than I can ever know. And I will never allow my silence to fail you ever again."

"Your silence allows us to sit here now, tonight, knowing that he is dead and buried and we can now give our people the safety and freedom they are owed."

Gideon smiled, "And does my queen argue so vociferously against her own doubts?"

No, she did not. But she'd felt every death during those years as if she'd ordered it herself. "I don't know why I argue with you. You always have a way of making me want to agree with you."

"Then don't argue with me," he pointed out, the corners of his eyes crinkling. "Just agree. You should be kinder to yourself, my queen. I know you wish to destroy every draconian law your husband ever created, but it will not happen today. Or tomorrow. Or even within the year. Inch by inch, we take this country back to the promise it once had."

"We?" she asked, a little flirtatiously.

Gideon's lashes obscured his eyes. "*We*. For the council stands at your side, prepared to do your every bidding."

Alexandra smuggled a secret little smile. For she understood he wasn't speaking of the council at all. "Perhaps you are right then. Perhaps I should allow myself this one night of freedom. What would you suggest?"

"Chess," he said immediately. "I may even allow you to win."

"*Allow?*" How dared he?

Gideon laughed under his breath. "I'm going to pay for that, am I not?"

"I will destroy you," she vowed.

"Sir Gideon?" Alexandra called. "A word with you, if I may?"

Gideon's gaze slowly lifted to hers, as the rest of the council filed out through the door. He'd been half-turned to follow the others, but paused at her imperious words.

She glanced at the others, but Malloryn was deep in conversation with Barrons and didn't pause. A little thrill ran through her at the thought of concocting a seduction beneath his very nose. Everyone knew she and Sir Gideon were friends—they often played chess together—but hopefully nobody suspected there was more between them.

"As you wish," he said with a polite bow of the head, and made his goodbyes to the rest of the council.

The door closed, leaving them both alone.

"I have had some thoughts on your proposal," she said firmly, knowing Malloryn wasn't out of earshot. "I would like to discuss it in private at some length."

"*Some length?*" he mouthed, shaking his head at her.

Alexandra dragged her fingertip across the polished surface of the dining table, smiling a little dangerously. "Indeed. Would you care for that game of chess now, while I gather my thoughts?"

"I could spare you an hour of my time," he teased. "Does this proposal have anything to do with the Scandinavian summit, or does it refer to another alliance?"

"Oh, Gideon." She rolled her eyes. "We were discussing the precise treaty I wish to speak of the other day—a meeting of strong-willed forces and a potential alliance between the two. It may take more than an hour."

"My night is at your disposal, Your Majesty."

He followed her through the door into the hallway that led to her private chambers. A maid curtsied, then darted into the dining room behind them as Alexandra strode along the carpets.

There was no sign of the council.

The second they were through the door into her drawing room, he captured her wrist and brought her hand to his mouth. "Is this the alliance you were referring to?"

"Perhaps. Though it depends upon whether a satisfactory trade agreement can be reached. What do you have to offer?"

"Pleasure," he whispered, brushing his lips against the inside of her wrist. "Worship." His tongue lashed against her pulse. "Absolute adoration."

Desire surged through her—not simply desire for him physically, but a yearning to break free of the prison she'd somehow placed herself in.

It had been one thing to congratulate herself on how well she'd been managing.

Three years without succumbing.

But three years abstaining did not mean she'd spent those years living.

He'd been right. She was too hard on herself. Ever since the revolution, she'd been forcing herself to live an abstemious life, working from dawn to dusk to try and compensate for the guilt she felt.

But perhaps it was time to remove that heavy weight from her shoulders.

"Kiss me," she demanded, sliding her hand through his hair and hauling his face down to hers.

Show me what it's like to live. To feel.

"As my queen commands."

His breath scoured her lips as he lowered his face. Capturing her face in both hands, he brushed the faintest of kisses across her mouth. Sweet. Sensual. Both a tease and a seduction. The tip of his tongue darted out, brushing against hers, and then she was lost.

"More," she breathed, curling her fist in his hair and wilting against him.

The kiss deepened.

Unlike their first embrace, Gideon did not take. Nor did

he demand. Every stroke of his tongue was an invitation, his hands playing a masterful tune on her body. He brushed his thumbs against her cheeks, her lips, her chin. The trace of his fingertips grazed their way down the column of her throat as if he was slowly learning every inch of her.

It surprised her to learn that such mere touches—feather light and upon her neck, no less—drove a shiver all the way through her.

Alexandra felt soft and heavy, her skin flushing with heat. She wanted to lean into him. All the way in. To rub herself against the soft wool of his coat and perhaps slide her hands beneath it—

And why not?

She grew daring, earning the soft intake of breath from him as she explored. Every inch of him was firm with muscle. She couldn't help herself. Capturing his mouth, she started tugging at his shirt, wanting to run her nails across his skin, wanting to linger in the heat that welled beneath his flesh.

"Alexa."

She kissed the protest away. Obliteration. That was all she sought. Let it all sweep away, hazy on the river of desire coursing through her.

"Alexa." Gideon broke free, thrusting one hand against the door at her back in order to restrain himself. His breathing came hot and heavy, and desire darkened his eyes. "What has brought this on?"

"Perhaps I'm tired of enduring. Perhaps I want to *feel*."

He avoided her grasp and captured her hand, nuzzling at her fingers. "Alexa. Alexa. Stop. Slow down."

She didn't want to slow. She wanted obliteration.

But he captured her face between his calloused palms and pressed a gentle kiss to her forehead. "I know you," he whispered. "Something else is driving this."

She pushed away from him, pacing the room in a swirl of skirts. "Must it be anything more than lust?"

"I don't know," he replied, crossing his arms over his chest. "Why don't you tell me?"

Alexandra's fingers curled into a fist. "I don't want to talk. I want to kiss you. I want you to kiss me."

"My queen does not always get what she desires."

Sometimes she wanted to scream. "Clearly." Pacing across the rug, she rubbed both hands down the silk of her skirts. "What do you suggest instead?"

"Talk to me," he insisted, crossing to the shelves and reaching for the chess set they often played with. "And then we shall negotiate terms on how far the night will go."

How far...?

Alexandra paused. She wanted to burst with frustration. "You are the most vexing man," she sputtered.

Gideon cocked his head. "I am a patient man. Not a vexing one. And you are not ready for more between us. Not like this. I want you, Alexandra. And I will have you. But I know your moods, and I will not be mere distraction for whatever is plaguing you. If you do not wish to discuss it, then there are other means to pass the time. Black or white?"

"White, curse you."

She would not give him the satisfaction of knowing that perhaps he was right.

"As you wish."

CHAPTER 11

Hours ticked past, and her gaze kept shifting to the clock impatiently.

Gideon's heated gaze lifted to hers as he took his king and set it directly to the side of her queen. He seemed to be enjoying making her wait. "King takes queen."

Alexandra swept her palm across the board, letting all the remaining pieces tumble to the floor. "I think the issue is clearly that this *king* is not taking this queen."

He smiled faintly as he poured himself another glass of cordial. He knew her abstemious nature and refused to drink in front of her. "I wouldn't presume. I am no king, my dear."

"You seem remarkably unambitious for someone who has a queen waiting upon him."

Gideon paused as he picked up the chess pieces. "To be named consort has never been my ambition."

The words made her falter.

"No?" She gave a careless shrug, but she felt the blow.

He looked up from where he knelt beside the small table. "I have never desired power for power's sake. You know that."

"So, you're the only man in England who does not desire to marry me?"

"I didn't say that." He dumped all the chess pieces in the box and snapped it shut. "You are an amazing woman. Despite all that you have lost, you have always sought to give your people the best you could manage. You have fought for them, suffered for them, and all because you see yourself not as subjugator but as subject, bound to serve your people. I have long been in awe of you. Any man would be honored to be your husband. Not because of what you could offer him, but for what you gift him with your mere presence." He paused, then growled under his breath. "Your husband will be a lucky man."

She couldn't quite meet his gaze.

"If I can bring myself to take one."

Moving toward her, he knelt on the edge of the divan, the neat pressed line of his slacks tightening over his thigh. Alexandra sucked in a sharp breath, a little thrill shivering over her skin.

"I would say you are progressing nicely," he murmured. "You nearly stole my virtue against the door of the drawing room."

"You're hardly an innocent, Gideon."

His lashes lowered in a dark curtain over his eyes as his gaze dropped to her lips. "I'm forty-three. I have learned a trick or two in my time."

"Such an old man," she teased.

"A wise man who knows you should be wooed."

"Your definition of the word appears to be dissimilar to mine."

"Does it?" He captured her hand, his thumb rasping across the delicate skin on the back of it. "You fear physical intimacies. Why, then, would I force them? I merely meant to allow you time to relax."

Alexandra swallowed. "Does not my desire speak for itself?"

"Is it desire that drives your urgency? Or fear? Fear you will never be able to allow yourself physical surrender?"

His words struck her to the core.

"I do not want you desperate," he said. "I want you to be certain. I want you to be comfortable. I want you to feel cherished. I can wait, Alexandra."

But could she?

"If I cannot bring myself to bear such intimacies now," she whispered, "then will I ever be able to? My physicians are already concerned about my advanced age."

He kissed her palm, pressing her hand to his cheek for a long second while she swallowed down the pain.

"Curse your physicians. There are nearly ten years between us. You make *me* feel old, at times."

"*Wise*," she teased, stroking his cheek. Her smile faded. "You always know my mind, even before I myself know it."

"I know *you*. I know your fears, because I want to protect you from them. I know your worries, because I want to share them."

Alexandra took in a deep breath. "Has a queen ever known such fealty?"

Gideon slowly looked up. "It was never fealty, Alexa. Fealty implies a debt, and what I would give you is everything, and willingly."

She looked away. His confession was too much. "Even if…."

"Always," he promised. "No matter what may come, you will always have my heart. It was gifted to you long ago, and I may never take it back."

She pressed her forehead to his. What she would not give to be able to look the council in the eye and tell them she had made her choice.

But what would the cost be?

A human queen with a human consort? And not only human, but one of the progressives, pushing for more rights for those of his species. The very thing that made her love him was the thing that separated them. Malloryn would have no truck with it. The Echelon would be furious. She'd only barely managed to pull London back together after Lord Balfour's reign of terror, and the last thing she needed was the blue blooded aristocrats rising up in force again.

There would be riots. There would be blood in the streets.

If she married Gideon, then more of her people would die.

"You have never made me resent my country so much," she whispered.

He had no reply to that.

Only the knowledge in his dark eyes that echoed hers. This was all they could have. Stolen moments. Stolen kisses. Secret confessions.

And she'd wasted enough of their short time together as it was.

Tilting her face to his, she closed her eyes and surrendered to the kiss he promised. Their lips met. A gentle brush. Alexandra clasped his face between her hands, leaning into the embrace. He kissed her softly, reverently. He kissed her as if their days weren't numbered, long and lazy and slow, until she was barely breathing.

The fire crackled behind her.

Gideon pushed up onto his knees, tumbling her back onto the divan. Pressing one knee between her thighs, he crawled over her, resting on his knuckles.

"Does my queen wish to be taken?" he whispered, brushing the edge of her gown off her shoulder.

Good lord. The barest touch and it set her on edge as nothing else might. "Your queen wishes for you to stop bloody talking and use that mouth for good cause."

Another smile. Curse him.

"Does she?" He leaned down, turning his face into her ear

as he brushed the backs of his fingers across her bare shoulder. "But my hands do marvelous things too."

The words whispered across the sensitive skin of her throat as he brushed his face against her cheek. The rasp of his stubble earned a gasp from her. Gideon was kind and thoughtful in all matters, but she hadn't expected to gain such pleasure from his slow, gentle restraint. It felt like an exquisite sort of torture.

"Lie back," she ordered.

He surrendered to her request, reclining against the daybed. Every inch of him was ruffled, from his hair to his shirt to his trousers. But there was still some mysterious sense of command he never truly seemed to lose.

She plucked at his buttons, baring inch by erotic inch of him and looking her fill. The sight of all that hair shocked her. His skin was almost olive in comparison to her husband's, and a thick thatch of hair decorated the heavy slab of his chest and the smooth barrel of his abdomen. In all her imaginings of him, she'd never quite pictured this.

She didn't know where to put her hands.

She didn't know what to do next.

"Why stop there?" he purred.

"Because—" Shyness consumed her.

Reaching up, he tugged a lock of hair free from her chignon, sliding it over and around his fingers.

Gideon reached down and flipped open the placket of his trousers. His cock surged erect behind it, though he left the fabric tented over the suggestion of him. "I ache for you. It aches for you." Taking himself in hand, he slowly pumped his fist up and down the full length of himself. "Don't make me beg."

"What do you want of me?"

"Touch me."

And so she did.

At first it was a gentle exploration. More curiosity than

anything else. But the soft sounds he made drew her into the act, and she found herself watching his face. Gideon always seemed so in control of himself, but she could sense the fine tremors beneath his skin as he tried to hold himself back.

And that would not do.

She leaned down to kiss him, and he met her mouth eagerly. Cupping a hand around hers, he showed her how to work his body, and Alexandra found herself melting against him. A languorous heat slid through her veins like molten honey. Power. This was power. And he'd surrendered himself to her. It seemed an aphrodisiac like no other.

She kissed his chin, and he tilted his head up, revealing his throat.

Another little display of vulnerability, and she found she liked it.

"More," he demanded, and she bit him, her blunt teeth sinking into the muscle where his neck met his shoulder.

Gideon's eyes darkened as she kissed her way down his abdomen, pausing to explore. Hands and mouth and tongue.... He liked that best, she thought. And he liked her mouth upon him, she was swiftly learning.

"Alexa." His hands tangled in her hair, and he tried to tug her up.

"No," she said, shaking his hand away.

"Tell me what you want."

"I want to not be afraid of this," she whispered, and then she lowered her head and kissed the smooth skin just above his trousers.

She could have sworn Gideon stopped breathing.

"I think *I'm* afraid you'll stop." He tried to sound teasing, but he didn't dare move, she noticed.

"I do recall someone teasing me almost to the point of mindfulness, and then ceasing." Alexandra looked up, reveling in this small role as temptress.

"Don't you dare."

"Beg me," she whispered.

His arms quivered, and the muscles in his abdomen tightened as he lifted his head off the daybed to watch what she was doing. "If you think that I'm—"

She trailed her tongue across the ridge of his pelvic bone, her passion-loosened hair dragging across his erection.

"Fuck." Gideon collapsed back on the daybed. "Curse you. Don't stop."

She shook her head, dragging her lips across that sensitive strip of skin. Back and forth. Back and forth. "So demanding, Gideon."

It was easy to feel relaxed with such gentle banter. Her nervousness washed away, and she nudged the flap of fabric out of the way. Gideon sucked in a sharp breath, his entire body splayed for her view.

Good lord. She'd thought the size of him excessive in her earlier explorations, but this….

The first brush of her lips to his swollen cock stole a gasp from him.

"Hell and ashes," he gasped, writhing before her.

What a strangely delightful act.

"More," he demanded, and thrust his hips up so that the tip of him breached her mouth.

This was new territory, but she set out to conquer it as one did when one was queen.

"Alexa," he gasped, his hands trembling on her head. "Alex, damn it. I can't— I'm going to—" His fingers curled into her hair. And then his hips were thrusting up, and she almost choked. "Oh God. I can't stop."

And then his hands were pressing her down, encouraging her to swallow more of him.

It didn't bother her. Indeed, she relished the feeling of power, the quiver of his body as he gasped and begged for mercy. She could feel him shaking with the need to surrender, feel him fighting it.

And failing.

"Alexa," he warned, throwing his head back on her mattress. "I can't stop."

In answer, she dragged the full length of her tongue up him and sucked the swollen head of his member.

Hot seed spilled into her mouth as he bucked beneath her. His hands curled into fists in her hair, and an utterly un-Gideon-like cry echoed.

"Dear God," he breathed as he collapsed back upon the pillow. "Dear God."

Gideon lay flat on his back, one arm thrown over his eyes.

Alexandra sat up, wiping her lips. The experience had been both heady and fulfilling, but she didn't know what to do now.

You just pleasured him like a bawd.

And she'd enjoyed every moment of it.

"Gideon?" she whispered, for he wasn't moving, and he hadn't said a word beyond "Dear God."

He swatted her with one of the cushions. "I cannot believe you just did that."

"Nor can I."

Capturing her in his arms, he rolled her onto the daybed. Alexandra caught at his shoulder, momentarily startled, and it took her a moment to realize she felt no fear at the sudden move.

Not with him.

She landed flat on her back, drowning in a spill of her skirts.

"My turn," he said, in a smoky voice as he lowered his head to her bodice.

She could feel the press of his thigh between hers, forcing her knees to part, and the weight of his body. It no longer unnerved her—this was Gideon, after all—but she still felt unsettled.

His lips brushed against her breast, and then his hand was

in her skirts, sliding them up. Tension warred in her belly, the *yes* and the *no* twisting her into knots, and then the roughness of his stubble was marking her skin and his hot mouth found her nipple.

Too much.

Far too much.

That hand slid up her thigh, and a part of her wanted him to continue—a part of her desperately wanted to be able to lie back and surrender, but there was also that tiny, tremulous piece of her that quavered at the thought.

"No," she said, pushing him away.

Gideon froze. "Did I hurt you?"

"*No.*" She scrambled out from beneath him, her breath coming in faint hitches. "No, it's not…. It's…. It's not necessary," she told him, shaking out her skirts as she stood.

"Not necessary?" Shock reigned rampant in his voice as he sat up, his trousers unbuttoned and his shirt in disarray.

Alexandra strode toward the doorway. "You've done as I asked. I no longer find myself frightened of the male physique. Anything else is… simply excessive." She paused by the door, taking one last look back at him. "Thank you."

"Alexandra!"

But she was already gone.

GIDEON WATCHED THE DOORS SLAM SHUT BEHIND HER, HIS HEART thumping into the bottom of his rib cage like lead before he shook off his stupor.

Not necessary, my ass.

Launching to his feet, he swiftly buttoned his trousers and then went after her.

The queen had not yet made her escape when he barreled through the doors to her drawing room.

The second she heard the doors slam behind her, she

flinched, whirling on him with her fists balled. A flash of fear darkened her eyes before she tipped her chin up, but it made him slam to a halt as nothing else would.

"This discussion is over," she told him.

"Because you say it is?"

"I'm the queen," she told him imperiously. "So, yes, it's over because I say it is."

"Hogwash," he said, taking a step toward her. "You're afraid, and you're running away from whatever it is that frightens you. Talk to me, Alexa. Please. Help me understand."

Emotion warred upon her face.

She never liked to be vulnerable, he knew.

"Did I frighten you?" he pleaded. He moved, blocking her escape but not putting hands on her. "Why will you not let me pleasure you? Was it my touch?"

The queen's face flushed. "Because I don't need that. An heir does not require that I be touched. It's just... thrusting. And if I'm no longer afraid, then I can manage that. It's not your touch. It's too much. I used to... I used to imbibe milk of poppy before he came to me. And I could tolerate it, if I could drift through it. But when you touch me, it feels as though my nerve endings are alight. As though I'm on the verge of losing control."

Violence spilled through him, inarticulate and furious. If the bastard wasn't dead, he'd have murdered the prince consort with his bare hands.

Instead, he pressed a hand to the side of her hip. "No, begetting an heir doesn't require pleasure, but you should demand it. You should know it at least once in your damned life."

Her eyes snapped fire. "Who are you to deem what I should and shouldn't know?"

No one. I am no one. His lips pressed firmly together. "I

thought we were in this together? I thought this was a partnership?"

"You're complaining because I will give you pleasure but won't accept it?" she scoffed. "What sort of man are you?"

One who loves you.

One who wants every piece of you, even as you deny him.

But again, he could not say it.

Instead, he was forced to yield, lowering his forehead to hers. "I am not the sort of gentleman who leaves a lady wanting. You damn me to be selfish, Alexandra, and I will not have it."

"Will not have it?"

"Will not," he said sternly.

The breath came out of her in a rush.

So. Not as unaffected as she claimed.

He brushed the backs of his fingers down her cheek. "Let me, Alex. Let me love every inch of you. Let me worship you and show you what it can be like between a man and a woman."

Closing her eyes, she slowly nodded.

Gideon kissed her. Soft, gentle kisses that stoked and stirred. He sensed the moment she began to kiss him back, surrendering to her fate.

Pressing her back against the door, he trailed his lips down her throat. Her breasts lifted as she inhaled, her hazel eyes glittering with suppressed need as he worked his way down her body. Finally he was kneeling on one knee at her feet, his hands sliding beneath her green skirts. Looking up, he slowly slid his hands up her stockinged calves.

Alexandra shivered.

But she did not look away.

Every inch of her looked regal, but there was a sense of vulnerability about her. A woman daring to pursue passion for the first time. Lifting her foot, he braced it on his thigh.

Her skirts tumbled over the pair of them as his hands began their slow caress.

"What are you doing?" Her voice rose.

"Kneeling as supplicant," he told her. "So I can worship my queen."

"Gideon!" she gasped.

"The first time I saw you, I could not look away," he whispered, toying with the silk ribbon of her garters. He tugged one loose. "You were the most beautiful woman I'd ever seen. You stared the prince consort in the eye in the middle of court and told him to damn his blood taxes. They were not going to rise."

Alexandra's lips parted. "They did rise."

"Slowly," he whispered. "But I never forgot your defiance. I looked at you, and for the first time in my life I knew there was hope for the realm."

Pressing a kiss to the inside of her knee, he breathed in the scent of her.

"You inspired me," he admitted. "You were so brave. And I spent years wishing I had half your bravery."

Capturing her thighs, he pushed them apart. A tremor ran through her, but as their eyes met, he realized it wasn't one of fear, but of desire.

He kissed his way up her thighs, encouraged by the way she threw her head back. The rasp of her breath filled his ears, and he deliberately dragged his stubbled cheek across her inner thighs.

"Gideon." Her fingers tangled in his hair. "Gideon, what are you doing to me? Oh. *Oh.*"

He rubbed his face against her drawers, his tongue finding the seam. The silk was wet with her musk, and she cried out as he parted the seam of her drawers and found the secret heart of her. Curling his palms under her ass, he tugged her toward his mouth, and then plunged his tongue inside her.

"Oh!" Her cry rent the air, and he caught a glimpse of her flushed cheeks and startled eyes. "Gideon! What are you—?"

Enough. Enough talk. Enough protest.

He kissed her wetly, driving his tongue into the slick heat of her body as she cried out again. Fingers curled in his hair, shocked cries filling the antechamber.

The musky taste of her body was exquisite. But the quiver of her thighs—the uncontrolled clenching of her fingers—almost undid him.

This was Alexandra laid bare, all her guarded trappings stolen from her, as she was forced to surrender to him.

This was his queen, the woman he loved, and damn him for a fool, but if he never had the chance to touch her again, he'd ensure that both of their memories were branded with every second of this encounter.

She came with a cry, her body wilting against the door. "What have you done to me?"

Wiping his mouth, he pushed to his feet and swept her into his arms. "I have barely begun."

CHAPTER 12

Kincaid pushed open the door to the mechanical jewelers, glancing up to check that this was the right address. "Think there's anyone here?"

Charlie followed on his heels, coughing under his breath at the dust that had been dislodged. "Shopkeepers rarely leave their wares unattended. And if they do, then they're not long in business. Judging from the dust on these shelves, this fellow's been around since the time of my great-grandfather."

Shelves lined the shop, filled with all manner of mechanical trinkets. A feathered parrot watched them from a cage, an automaton's head stared glassily at him as Kincaid bent low to peruse the shelves, and several metal gauntlets lay covered with dust. He flexed his metal hand, staring at the gauntlets. "He's a mech," he said, judging the work. "Ironmonger enclaves, by the look of it."

"A mech creating jewelry?"

"I don't think he does the cutting of the gems." Kincaid looked around. "No, this fellow's the one who created that beacon, and most likely those gyrfalcons."

Movement shifted.

"What's that?" Charlie seemed jumpier than a cat in a factory full of mousetraps.

Metal clanked on metal, and Kincaid relaxed as he heard the familiar sound of pistons moving mechanical joints. "It's a servant drone."

But what emerged from behind the shelves was not merely a drone, but the upper body of a mechanical man, welded to the bottom half of a spider. A bowler hat was welded to the creature's head, and someone had put a coat and tie on him, but there was no disguising the long spars of the spider's leg.

Even Kincaid's eyebrows hit his hairline.

"What the hell is that?" Charlie asked.

"I ain't ever seen the like."

The drone's mouth fell open. "Welcome to MacGregor's House of Curiosities. Mr. MacGregor will be with you shortly."

"I think it's the reason the door is unlocked and yet the owner is unafraid any of his wares'll go missing." Quite frankly, Kincaid couldn't take his eyes off the creature. He'd seen automatons programmed to respond to a series of set questions, but this thing actually appeared to be staring at him.

Both of them remained frozen.

"Do you think it can hear us?" Charlie hissed.

"Please take a seat," the drone replied. "Mr. MacGregor will be with you shortly."

Indeed, Kincaid could just make out footsteps climbing the old stairs in the back of the shop. "Mr. MacGregor?"

A pair of googly eyes emerged, surrounded by a cap of wiry hair. "Aye," the fellow said, pushing his expanding goggles up on top of his head. "What you want?" He eyed them from top to toe. "You ain't here to shop. I've paid me licenses, I have. Just last month."

"We're not regulators, Mr. MacGregor," Charlie said,

holding out a hand. "We're investigators."

"Nighthawks, eh?" MacGregor stomped behind his counter, pulling a flask out from beneath it and taking a mouthful. "What you want? I ain't got nothin' to hide."

For a man with nothing to hide, he was certainly acting a little unhappy to see them, though Kincaid didn't correct the Nighthawk presumption.

He pulled the wreckage of the scarab beacon out of his coat pocket. Half of it was melted into slag, but the rest was very clearly the ass end of the jewel, with half its wires hanging out.

"We'd like to ask you a few questions about this little thing. And just how one of your devices ended up in a room where the queen was nearly killed."

"Your Majesty."

The words echoed through the portrait hall. Alexandra stilled. She'd been hoping to find her apartments and have a private cup of tea. Everywhere she looked these days, there was someone hounding her for attention.

"Prince Ivan," she said, turning around slowly. Her ladies-in-waiting caught her eye, and she dismissed them with a nod. "What a pleasure."

"You are well?" he demanded, striding toward her. "The Duke of Malloryn said someone tried to kill you. And they used my brooch to do it!"

"I am fine," she told him. He always seemed so emotional, and she was growing a little weary of placating him. "We were lucky that the Duke of Malloryn was in the room with me and was able to defend me."

He knelt at her feet. "I did not know, Your Majesty. I thought it was just a brooch. Just a gift. I did not realize I was being played for a fool."

"Have you remembered who directed you to that particular jeweler?"

The prince looked up, a stricken cast to his face. "As I tell your duke, no. She was just another lady at court. I pay them little attention."

He paid them enough attention, she had noticed, though she did not doubt the truth of his words. He wasn't the sort of man to focus on a lady's face when he was speaking to her.

"Please tell me you forgive me," he begged, capturing her hand.

"Of course I forgive you," she replied smoothly, wishing he would stand up. She was not given to such emotional displays.

He obeyed, surging to his feet with an alacrity that startled her, and took her hand. "I would never strike such a blow against you. I am here as an envoy from Russia, and I would never place my country's fate in such jeopardy. Nor would I dare risk a hair on your head."

"Of course not."

He pressed her hand to her face. "I take presumptions again, but I've barely been able to sleep or think since I heard the news. I would hate for you to think me guilty, after all we've shared."

"Prince Ivan—"

He kissed her.

Alexandra stilled, but it was not as immediately disgusting as she'd originally feared. Though certainly not as sweet as Gideon's kisses.

She didn't know what to do. Prince Ivan was clearly interested in pursuing an alliance. And ties to Russia could prove beneficial. There was a wealth of trade treaties to explore.

And no other prince or duke here for the exhibition had pursued her with as much fervor. Though his presence didn't make her heart flutter, she felt he could have been managed. A parade of mistresses through his bed would keep him distracted whilst she ruled the realm, and they would only occasionally have reason to come together.

This alliance could be good for Britain.

Ivan's kiss deepened, as if he'd expected her to push him away immediately.

She set her hands to his chest, intending to do just that.

Footsteps slowed, and a shocked gasp echoed through the parlor just as Alexandra sought to escape Ivan's tongue. She pushed away from Prince Ivan in a flurry, only to find her lover standing in the doorway.

The shock on Gideon's face scalded her.

"Gideon—"

He swiftly masked the heavy emotion she'd seen. "My apologies. I was not aware there was anyone in this wing." Bowing his head, he stepped away from her, and she hated the way he would not meet her eyes. "I shall leave you to… to it."

"Gideon." She started after him, but he was practically fleeing down the hallway, his long legs eating up the rugs and his coattails flaring behind him.

Her hand lowered as she noted the hunched way he held his shoulders. She'd hurt him. He knew she was being courted by another man, her future offered to another, but it was one thing to know it, quite another to see it.

She felt ill.

What was she going to do? Prince Ivan had clearly displayed his intentions. Russia would be a good match for her empire.

But every inch of her heart demanded she chase Sir Gideon and try to explain.

"I think perhaps that now he will know I am not merely a *friend* to the queen." Prince Ivan wore a satisfied smile as he stepped beside her, placing a hand on the small of her back and rubbing there.

She wanted to scream.

CHAPTER 13

The queen stared into space as she lounged in her bath.

What was she going to do? Prince Ivan had displayed his intentions quite clearly, and Gideon— Gods, Gideon. She couldn't help seeing his face again, as he came across another man kissing her. She hadn't seen him since, no matter how much she'd searched for him. It made her feel ill.

Water suddenly cascaded over her head and shoulders.

Alexandra sputtered, and hauled herself upright. "Are you trying to drown me?"

Mina rested her bottom on the edge of the bath, lowering the jug. "I was washing your hair. It's not my fault you're distracted. I warned you. Twice."

Alexandra subsided with a thin press of her lips. "You voted for me to take a husband, so technically, it *is* your fault. What did you expect?"

"You've blithely ignored all your suitors," Mina replied, handing Alexandra a washcloth. "And yet you're clearly mooning after someone. I will confess, I've never quite seen you like this."

"I'm not mooning after anyone," Alexandra snarled.

Mina arched a brow which said, quite clearly, what she

thought of that statement. "I thought we kept no secrets from each other?"

"That was before you cast me to the devil."

"I thought you'd forgiven me for my vote?"

Alexandra looked away. It wasn't Mina's fault that the day's events had happened as they had. Guilt festered within her, and though she knew she was lashing out unfairly, she couldn't quite bring herself to apologize.

Mina knelt beside the tub, taking Alexandra's hand between hers. "Who is it that causes you such consternation?"

She sighed and collapsed back against the bath. "Prince Ivan was virtually down on one knee today." She pressed a hand to her lips, feeling again that lackluster kiss and wishing she could replace it with Gideon's. "As ruling monarch, I must be the one to officially ask for his hand, but I know what his answer will be."

"Prince Ivan?" Mina said noncommittally.

"He *is* a blue blood," she pointed out.

"What does it matter whether your future husband is a blue blood? A human would be acceptable."

Alexandra's heart skipped a beat.

"The Echelon would be up in arms. A human consort poses a risk, when I am a human queen. I need to choose someone whom the majority of London will accept. There's been so much unrest. Too much blood and tears. My people deserve peace and prosperity."

"Choosing a human consort isn't going to ignite a war," Mina countered. "And we will all understand why you wouldn't wish for another blue blood in your bed."

Alexandra stirred her legs through the water.

She felt almost breathless. Was it true?

"Do you truly think the Echelon would accept a human consort?"

"There are ways to manage them," Mina replied. "Set Malloryn upon the few rabble-rousers that remain."

"Malloryn? Good grief. I cannot risk alienating them. They're already terrified of him. And we've barely recovered from Lord Balfour's coup attempt. The peace is so tenuous."

She didn't dare do anything to risk it.

"Then let your council deal with it," Mina insisted. "That's what we are there for. To support you. There are many Great Houses who have lost their entire bloodline in the coup attempt. Estates stand empty and titles languish. There's nothing a blue blood aristocrat likes more than the opportunity to improve their standing. Gift a few estates that the crown holds in escrow. Knight a handful of loyal blue bloods. Dangle a duchy in front of some of the others... but only if they behave."

Could it be possible?

She'd been staring war in the face for so long that it had frozen her. The human and blue blood conflict had been so ingrained in the past few years that she'd felt as though she walked a narrow tightrope between them.

"The commoners would love a human consort," she said slowly. "And if I can manage the Echelon, it... it may be possible."

"Though not the Duke of Alba's brother," Mina teased. "Not if he cannot understand you."

"No? That sounds like the perfect husband to me. As long as we can conceive an heir, it doesn't matter whether I can speak to him or not. The more interests he has outside marriage, the better. This won't be a love match."

The words sounded almost by rote, but she couldn't help thinking of Gideon. Her heart quickened, and she hoped Mina didn't hear. Dearest friend or not, she couldn't betray her growing feelings toward him. Not just yet. It still felt so new, and so... tenuous.

After all, he'd told her to her face that he did not desire to be her consort. Even if the Echelon could accept it, would he deny her?

There was a leaden pit in the hollow of her abdomen.

Mina stroked a finger along her jaw. "All jests aside, may I suggest you marry the man who's been leaving these marks on your throat."

Alexandra slapped a hand to the skin there. Surely not.

Mina laughed as she pushed to her feet. "I thought so. Marry the one kissing you in private corners. You'll never regret it."

Morning dawned. The skies were bleak and gray, matching his mood.

Gideon scraped a weary hand over his jawline as he examined the room. Most of his trunks were packed and only a few items lay strewn across the bed. With a snap of his fingers he could summon a carriage and be on his way to Haver Hall, where he could retreat to lick his wounds.

It felt like cowardice to flee the city—parliament would be in session soon, and he was still head of the Humans First party—but he didn't think he could spend another minute in Kensington, knowing she was only mere feet away.

And knowing that another man would be stealing kisses in dark hallways.

I just need a few days away from her. A few days to accept her loss.

Except even at Haver Hall, there would be ghosts to haunt him.

The chess board where he and Alexandra had spent many an afternoon, while they waited for Malloryn to defeat Balfour. The gray mare that the queen had become quite partial to. The garden where they'd walked and talked for hours.

And the stone folly where he'd kissed her and been rebuffed.

"Curse her." He turned and reached for the letter she'd sent several hours ago, even though he knew its contents by heart.

Leave?

Or stay and fight?

But what had she meant?

GIDEON,

I NEED TO SPEAK WITH YOU. PLEASE SEEK A MEETING WITH ME AT *your earliest possible convenience.*

HER ROYAL MAJESTY,
Queen Alexandra

AND THAT WAS IT.

The formality of the letter made his heart sink.

Was she cutting ties with him? Did she wish to gently inform him that she'd accepted Prince Ivan's suit?

Or was the formality a means to hide her thoughts—and heart, hopefully—from those who might intercept such a letter?

A sharp rap came at the door.

"Come in," Gideon called, scrunching her letter in his fist.

His man of affairs appeared, impeccable in black. "Shall I have the carriage sent for, Sir Gideon?"

He still didn't know the answer to that. "I...."

Long seconds ticked out.

Hansen cleared his throat. "It's just... there seems to be quite a goings-on down in the courtyard. It may take some time to arrange matters, what with all the ruckus."

"Ruckus?"

"News, sir."

"What news?" he asked sharply.

Sympathy twisted Hansen's expression. Few knew of his affections, but Hansen was a loyal servant and no doubt he'd caught wind of his master's feelings. "There is talk among the servants that the queen is going to reveal some happy news by the end of the day. She sent for Prince Ivan an hour ago, and they are walking in the garden together. Alone. The entire palace is waiting to hear word of their conversation."

The floor fell out from under him.

Gideon slowly sank into an armchair. He couldn't even blame Alexandra for the void where his heart lay. He'd known she was destined for another. He'd known another man would end up with her hand—and hopefully her heart. She needed to marry.

And he could never be the one to take her to wife.

He was too human, his bloodlines virtually worthless. They had never stood a chance, and in his heart of hearts, he'd always known it.

But it was one thing to know it, and quite another to see it actually happening, right before his eyes.

"Sir?" Hansen murmured.

His fist curled around her letter. "Send for the carriages," he said brusquely. "And then I shall get you to deliver a letter for me."

One final goodbye to the woman he loved.

"YOUR HIGHNESS." MALLORYN LAY IN WAIT AS THE PRINCE stormed up the stairs onto the balcony.

Prince Ivan turned on him, his lip curling and one hand dipping to his side where a weapon no doubt lurked. "You had a hand in this, didn't you? What did you say to her?

What did you do? She was mine, I know she was mine! She was ready to surrender!"

Malloryn merely arched a brow. "If you think Her Majesty was prepared to propose to you, then you are a fool. Her Majesty does not *surrender*. Nor are her affections dictated by those around her. She is the Queen of Britain, and I am her servant, and nothing else. You would be wise to curb your tongue, for the sake of Britain and Russia's abiding friendship."

Ivan's lip curled. "Perhaps that friendship will endure. Though whether the queen does, is another matter entirely."

He moved to push past, but Malloryn grabbed his arm, his voice dropping to a lethal level. "What does *that* mean? Are you threatening Her Majesty?"

"Of course, I'm not. Do you think me a fool?" This time, it was Ivan's turn to smile as he reached out and straightened the lapels on Malloryn's coat. "I don't have to do a thing. All I have to do is watch. Britain will fall, torn apart from within, and Russia—"

He slammed the prince back against the wall, one second away from doing violence. "You skate treacherously close to ruin, Your Highness. Have a care. Because I swear to you, that if the queen falls, then I will do everything in my power to ensure you are blamed for it."

A hint of caution reared in Ivan's dark eyes. "My hands are clean."

"And yet, you know something. I'll consider that akin to playing part in a conspiracy."

Ivan curled his hands around Malloryn's and eased them from his coat. "I saw a familiar face today. Think about it, Malloryn. Who has the most to gain from the queen's death? Do you think they're going to stop just because their first two attempts were foiled?"

"Who is it?"

Ivan pushed him away with a faint smile. "Oh, I'll tell

you. But that will take time, Malloryn. And right now, the queen is alone. You should never leave her alone. Not here, in this pit of vipers. It's your choice. The truth? Or the queen's life?"

He froze.

Gemma was trailing Her Majesty today. And Gemma was his best.

But doubt niggled. All it would take would be one stray bullet. A blink from Gemma. A moment of distraction.

"Curse you." He started toward the gardens. "This conversation isn't finished."

Ivan smiled, as Malloryn reached the top of the stairs.

He almost slammed into Obsidian halfway down.

"The queen." Malloryn demanded. "Where is the queen?"

Obsidian frowned. "She was heading toward the stables. Why?"

"Because I think our killer's going to make another attempt."

SLIPPING AWAY FROM KENSINGTON PALACE UNSEEN WHEN ONE was the queen was impossible.

And stupid.

So Alexandra did neither.

Knowing Malloryn's spy was better at surveillance than Alexandra was at evasion, she simply ignored Miss Townsend and summoned a horse from the stables. Two of the Coldrush guards trailed her at a distance until it felt like she was leading a bloody parade, but at least it wasn't the entire court.

And after dozens of years of having her every move monitored, she ought to be used to it.

Rain dampened the morning, the skies gray and overcast.

It suited her mood. A pox on the whole damned court. A pox on the council. And a pox on Malloryn.

A particularly itchy one, preferably.

Urging her gray mare into a gallop, she let her mount fly across the grass of Hyde Park, the sting of rain lashing against her cheeks until she felt free for the first time in years.

It wasn't long enough. Ahead of her, an elaborate folly loomed out of the gardens, a curtain of icy drizzle near obscuring it.

Sir Gideon paced the folly, the black lash of his coattails betraying his mood. The second he saw her, he stilled.

There were no words.

Only the impenetrable, implacable black of his eyes.

"Say something." Alexandra lowered the hood of her cloak, shaking off the damp.

"What would my queen have me say?" he replied.

She held up the note he'd sent. "An explanation for this, if you would."

Gideon raked his hands through his hair, leaving it in unruly tangles. "I told you I cannot do this. I cannot stay and watch you marry another."

"And are you so certain I intend to marry another?" she asked sharply.

"Don't." His voice quavered. "Don't toy with my affections thusly."

She drew back angrily. "Do you think so little of me that you would think me so heartless?"

"Not heartless. No. But we both know how this ends. You are not at liberty to grant me anything more than your past affections. You are the queen. And Prince Ivan—"

"Is returning to Russia," she said heatedly. "He did not appreciate my rebuff of his suit."

Gideon froze. "You...."

"I told him that although our countries held great respect for each other, I could not accept his affections."

Gideon pinched the bridge of his nose. "You should have married him."

"*What?*"

"It was a sound alliance. He could have been managed as a consort, and Britain could have pursued some excellent trade agreements."

Alexandra drew herself up stiffly. "Trade agreements."

Did he not even care?

They stared at each other.

And her doubts grew.

All along she'd thought his humanity had been the point of contention. But what if there was more to it?

Gideon had said himself that he had no desire to be named consort. He was the head of the humanist movement, and if he married her, he would have to give up his political ambitions. The very thing that made her love him the most, was possibly the thing that might keep them apart.

Her confidence evaporated.

"So you will go? Just like that?" Her voice broke. "You promised. You promised you would never leave me."

"And I meant it. I will never leave you in here," he said, thumping a fist against his heart. "But I did not realize how it would feel to watch you kiss another man." His eyes grew anguished. "I cannot do this, Alexa. I cannot stand aside, not unless I am far away."

"Then don't." She caught his sleeve. "Don't stand aside."

"I cannot marry you."

"Says who?" she demanded. "Mina seems to think there is a way to manage the blue bloods. She seems to think I could marry a human. And your... your commitment to Humans First could be—"

"I'm not just human, Alexa. I am a no one. My father's grandfather was a baron. I'm not a prince. I'm not even a noble myself. I have so little aristocratic blood in my veins, it may as well not exist. I am virtually a commoner, Alexa. And you are a *queen*." He captured her face between his hands. "As for the party—"

She kissed him desperately, in order to still the words. Gideon froze, and then he captured her mouth with an anguished moan. All the things that couldn't be said spilled forth in a storm of passion. But even as their bodies meshed, she couldn't quite still her mind.

A tear slid slowly down her cheek as she realized this was very likely the last time they would ever embrace.

The urge to cast it all to the winds—duty, her commitment to the throne and her people—brewed within her like a stale batch of tea. Why could she not choose him?

Why could she not have just one thing for herself?

Alexandra broke the kiss, gasping for air.

"Stay," she begged, clinging to his coat and shaking her head. "I won't marry anyone else. I won't do it. We'll find a way. We could be lovers. We could take precautions. Elizabeth managed to rule by herself."

"Alexa." He carefully tugged her fingers free of their grip upon him, bringing them to his lips to kiss. The sadness in his eyes made the lump in her throat almost chokingly thick, for it held a "no." "You must marry. I see that now. And I want that for you. I want you to be happy. I want you to bear the children I cannot give you. And I will always think of you fondly. I will always be there if you should ever have need, but this... this needs to end. For both our sakes."

"And if I commanded you to stay?"

Gideon slowly stiffened. "I am bound to serve my queen."

But it would break him to do that, and it was only selfishness speaking. Her need for him overpowering her respect for this gentle, intelligent man.

Alexa swallowed hard, letting go of his hands.

She wasn't going to merely surrender. Not now. She just needed time to think her way through this mess.

"I will always love you," she whispered.

His gloved hands came up, brushing the tears from her cheek. "And I you."

A crack of distant thunder retorted.

Alexandra could bear it no longer. She tugged her hood up and swept away from him in a flurry of wet skirts, her eyes blinded by the tears she could no longer withhold.

And so, she did not see the figure step out of the bushes ahead of her, a pistol raised.

∽

"Well," Gemma said, huddling beneath an oak tree and blowing into her cupped hands. "It's a lovely day to be squiring Her Majesty around the countryside. I don't suppose anyone has a flask of hot toddy on them?"

The pair of Coldrush guards who waited with her glanced at each other.

"Tea?" she asked hopefully, trying to distract them from whatever was occurring within the folly.

As much as Malloryn would want to know all the details, the queen deserved a little privacy.

Judging from the guards' faces, there was no hot tea to be found. Only the wretchedly cold drizzle of water dripping from the lip of her cloak down the back of her neck.

"Well, dash it," she muttered, frowning a little as a strange sound caught her attention, something rhythmic and—

Hoofbeats echoed.

Gemma turned, palming her pistol and settling into a marksman's stance. Two riders approached, clods of earth flying up behind them as they thundered toward her. She took a half-step toward them before she recognized the aquiline intensity of Malloryn's expression and the broad shoulders of her lover.

"Gemma!" Malloryn yelled.

Instinct kicked into gear, and perhaps it was the urgency

in his expression or some strange sense, but she whipped around, bringing the pistol up—

A blur of movement whipped into view a half-second before something smashed into her face.

Gemma slammed into the ground, the pistol flying from her palm. Heat and pain obliterated her thoughts. She brought her hands up, curling into a ball to protect herself as a boot drove into her ribs.

One of the guards. Hit her with some kind of weapon.

A pistol retorted.

Gemma lurched to her hands and knees, her childhood training kicking in. The guard had lifted his weapon again, and she threw herself into a roll, half-disorientated and staggering badly as she came up. Blood and ashes. Where was her pistol? Where was the other guard?

Down. Dead. She saw that much.

Oh, heck.

The queen.

She had a split second to make a decision. Driving herself upright, she lurched under the strike and slammed the flat of her palm up into the guard's chin. His head snapped back, but she hadn't put as much force into it as she'd have liked.

The world spun, and his weapon—some kind of truncheon—smashed down across her shoulder, tearing a scream from her lungs.

The truncheon whipped back the other way, and Gemma rolled beneath it. Too late. She was backpedaling, on the wrong foot, trying to adjust to her injuries....

Pain hammered through her ear, and this time when she went down, she stayed there. Ears ringing. Blinking through the white lights glittering in her line of vision.

Move. Or die.

She heard Master Rickard's dry voice cracking through her memories. Saw again the line of children sparring in the

Falcon's training center, where she'd been forged into a child assassin.

Gemma rolled, biting her teeth against the pain. The guard took a menacing step toward her, then his gaze lifted and indecision flickered over his expression.

A shot ricocheted past.

Malloryn.

Obsidian wouldn't miss.

"Gemma!" Malloryn yelled.

The guard turned away from her, sprinting toward the folly. The queen. Damn it! Gemma scrambled for her fallen pistol, water dripping down her face and obscuring what little vision she had. Malloryn and Obsidian were still too far away, and whilst her lover could snipe a man from several hundred yards with a decent rifle, he was merely competent at riding.

"Your Majesty!" she screamed, grabbing the pistol and cocking it as she staggered into the tree, using it to brace herself.

In the folly, both the queen and Sir Gideon both looked up just as Gemma lifted the pistol.

It didn't matter.

She was going to be too late.

Because she wasn't the only one with a weapon, and her arm was shaking so badly she could barely aim the bloody thing.

The Coldrush guard lifted his own pistol, and she saw the queen's eyes widen in horror as she realized what was happening.

Her muzzle flashed, and Gemma knew instantly that her bullet hadn't flown true.

The Coldrush guard staggered, but his pistol retorted in echo to hers.

"No—"

A blur of movement slammed into the queen. Gemma

tried to lunge forward, but her ears were still ringing, and it felt like she was moving through treacle.

Sir Gideon and the queen crashed to the ground just as Malloryn arrived, flying past Gemma and launching himself out of the saddle at the guard. They fell in a crashing mess, rolling head over heels.

Malloryn could handle it.

Then Obsidian was at her side. "Are you all right?" he demanded, trying to help her to stand straight.

"The queen," she said breathlessly. She would never forgive herself if the queen died on her watch. How could she have been so stupid? As soon as she'd swept the perimeter and realized they were all alone out here in the park, she'd turned her back on the guard, lowering her vigilance for one precious second. Simply because she wanted the queen to have some privacy for her romantic rendezvous. She'd trusted a man she hadn't personally vetted, when she knew someone wanted to kill the queen.

Obsidian nodded and sprinted toward the queen.

Gemma staggered after him, her head still spinning, though she had her pistol cocked and reloaded.

Sir Gideon lay slumped over the queen, his breath coming in ragged pants. Blood flavored the air, and the queen didn't move.

"Is she hit?" Gemma demanded.

Obsidian hauled Sir Gideon off Her Majesty, his broad shoulders obscuring Gemma's line of sight.

"Damn it, is she hurt?"

"No." Obsidian looked up, his mouth tight. "It's not her blood."

And Gemma belatedly realized that the blur of movement had been the knight throwing himself at the monarch he loved.

"Oh, no," she whispered.

"Gideon!" the queen screamed, scrambling upright and pushing Obsidian away. "Gideon!"

And that was when Gemma saw the bloodied mess of the man's upper chest.

∼

"Gideon! Gideon!" Alexandra slid to her knees beside him.

Blood poured from the wound in his shoulder. The breath wheezed out of him as he tried to move. A terrible, whistling sound that drove a chill through her veins like liquid lead.

Alexandra tore his coat open, ignoring the restraining hands that sought to pry her away. "Curse you, leave me be!"

"It's not safe." Malloryn. Appearing out of nowhere.

She looked into his cold, gray eyes. "Then *make* it safe. I will not leave him."

Malloryn's cool gaze flickered to Gideon, and then he gave a curt nod. "Obsidian, set up a perimeter. Gemma, send for a surgeon. Immediately."

"Consider it done, Your Grace," said Miss Townsend.

Alexandra barely heard the words. All she could sense was movement behind her as Malloryn took charge.

Blood welled over her cupped hands as Sir Gideon gasped for breath. His dark eyes met her own, begging her for something she couldn't understand. He tried to grab her arm, but the movement was beyond him.

"No! Don't move." What was she going to do? She pressed her hands firmer, trying to hold his blood inside him from sheer pressure.

"Let me see," Malloryn said, kneeling at her side.

"I can't let go. I *can't*."

He caught her wrists, and their eyes met. "Trust me, Alexandra. Trust me. I need to see the wound."

Slowly, she let him move her hands away. Blood welled in sluggish lumps. There was so much of it.

"He's human," she whispered.

A blue blood could survive a wound like this, but Sir Gideon had been vaccinated against the craving virus. They couldn't even infect him now in order to save his life.

There was no emotion in Malloryn's eyes.

Only the cold, sharp assessment she was afraid to take herself as he pressed his cravat to the bleeding. "His lung is pierced. He doesn't have long."

"Do something," she begged. "Do something. *Please*."

Malloryn glanced down. "I *can't* infect him. My saliva may be able to heal some small components of this injury, but—"

All she heard was the "but."

All the warmth in the world washed away from her. *No*. She had lost everything—the father she'd adored, the mother who'd died at her birth, her youth, her innocence, her privacy, even her own choices. Sir Gideon was the one secret little pleasure she'd ever cherished. Her rock in any storm. Never trying to take from her, but standing at her side, always, there to tell her she wasn't alone when she faced difficult, terrible decisions.

She didn't think she could continue to rule without him.

Not without losing all sense of hope.

"I can help him." The tall, brooding man who always shadowed Miss Townsend pushed Malloryn out of the way. "The sac surrounding his lungs is filling with air and placing pressure on the lung itself. If we don't relieve some of that pressure it will collapse his lung completely, and he won't be able to breathe." He eased the bloodied cravat out of the way. "The bullet's still inside him, but it doesn't appear to have hit anything vital in itself."

Malloryn moved aside. "Will he survive, Obsidian?"

"Perhaps."

Perhaps? "Just what sort of experience do you have, sir? Are you a surgeon?"

The man's ghostly-pale eyes flickered to hers. *Dhampir*,

Malloryn had told her once. An enemy who had defected to their side. And now Sir Gideon's life lay in his hands.

"Usually I'm the one dealing such wounds," he replied matter-of-factly. Tugging a small leather satchel from within his coat, he rolled it out, revealing an array of wicked-looking instruments. "But I wouldn't have missed the heart if I'd taken that shot. Unless I meant to. Your Majesty, I think you should look away."

Alexandra shook her head, but Malloryn was already bustling her away from Sir Gideon's panting, wheezing body.

"Malloryn!" she gasped, trying to see over his shoulder.

"Here," he whispered, drawing her into his arms and forcing her tear-stained face into his shoulder. "Don't look," he whispered, the palm of his hand cupping the base of her skull. "He will survive it, Alexandra. I swear he will. He won't want to leave you. Just don't look, and it will all be over soon."

CHAPTER 14

Malloryn moved slowly around Sir Gideon's bedchambers, picking up one of the man's jackets—slung carelessly over a chair—before draping it over the queen's shoulders.

She sat by the bed, holding one of Sir Gideon's hands, her face pale and tearstained. Looking up in shock, she realized who the jacket belonged to, and then drew it close around her shoulders.

"You need to bathe and get out of that bloody dress," he murmured. "I'll send for some tea and supper for you to have in your rooms."

"I'm not going anywhere."

He bit off the words he was about to say, meeting his wife's eyes. Adele nodded, kneeling by the queen's side and taking her other hand.

"Your Majesty, you are wet to the skin and suffered a great shock today. You cannot watch over Sir Gideon if you take ill. And I am certain he would not wish you to put yourself at risk. I will sit with him while you bathe," Adele promised. "I'll make sure he's not alone."

The queen opened her mouth as if to argue, then glanced

at Gideon's face. "Please," she whispered. "Please come and fetch me if his circumstances take a turn."

"I will send one of the maids immediately," Adele promised.

Malloryn bustled her into the arms of her ladies-in-waiting before pinching the bridge of his nose the second the door was closed behind her. "What a fucking catastrophe. I should never have let her go riding off alone with only two of her guards and Gemma."

"You cannot control everything, and how were you to know someone had gotten to one of the guards?"

"I should have known," he bit out. "I personally vetted them myself after Lord Balfour's attack." He scrubbed the back of his neck and paced the Aubusson rug. "If it wasn't for Sir Gideon, she'd be dead. But no, I wanted her to have a nice rendezvous with the man."

Adele sighed, wrapping her arms around him from behind. "You are not omnipotent, Auvry. You took every precaution you could have done with the knowledge you had. And both she and Sir Gideon are alive, and the physicians seem to think he will survive. Obsidian did most excellent work."

"We were lucky."

"Yes, we were lucky. And now you're not going to be doing anyone any favors wearing a hole in that rug." Adele turned him around, then straightened his coat. "The Duke of Malloryn does not wring his hands and bemoan the past. He does not wear his guilt like a cape. You made a mistake. Gemma made a mistake. The queen made a mistake. But there's no point waffling on about it."

"I am *not* wearing my guilt—"

"You're being practically Byronic, my love." Reaching up, she tweaked the front of his hair into a curl. "Careful now, or they'll start whispering at court about the single stoic tear they saw sliding down your cheek."

"I'm a blue blood. I cannot cry. I do not cry."

"No? Nor do you lament the past. You have the guard in the dungeons," she pointed out, "and you've not made a single comment about interrogating him."

"That's because Byrnes is doing so as we speak. He's a trifle irate with him, after catching a glimpse of what the bastard did to Gemma."

"And the prince?"

His face hardened. "Certainly knows more than he first claimed. Though Charlie was keeping an eye on him, and said he managed to slip into the city."

"Then find him and encourage him to tell you all about it. Now go and find out who paid that guard to murder his queen. And don't come back until you have found him."

Malloryn glared down at her. "I hate being managed."

Adele rolled her eyes and laughed. "Don't I know it."

But he kissed her on the cheek and made his way to the door to do as he'd been told. Adele was right. He was hovering over Sir Gideon's sickbed like a nursemaid. "Send for me if his condition changes. I shall see you tonight for dinner."

BYRNES LOOKED DISCONSOLATE BY THE TIME MALLORYN REACHED the dungeon.

"What's wrong?" he demanded.

"See for yourself." Byrnes swung the door open.

Inside the cell, a man hung from the ceiling, his face purple. Malloryn swept the room with a glance, then gestured for Byrnes to shut the door. "What the hell happened? You allowed him a length of rope?"

"Do I look like some sort of amateur, Your Grace?"

Malloryn surveyed him again. "No." Generally speaking, when it came to information-gathering, he would have preferred to use Gemma—who had an absolute knack for stealing secrets from a man without having to even touch him—but Byrnes was no slouch. And he didn't make mistakes like this. "What happened?"

Byrnes held up his gloved fingers, revealing a slip of paper between them. "Use the rope," he read, "or your wife and son will make its acquaintance instead." He tsked under his breath. "We are dealing with some coldly calculating killers, Your Grace. I don't know how the letter got to him, but I found it in his pocket. Could have been any of the guards—"

"Search them."

"Our dear Kincaid is already doing so. The rope is another matter." Byrnes opened the door again and pointed to a small grate in the wall. "I believe it was slipped through the grate, though the opening into the air vents is so small that only a child would be able to move about within. Whoever it was, they're long gone. I left him alone for half an hour to think about... the choices he needed to make, and when I returned he was hanging."

Malloryn pinched the bridge of his nose. "So, my suspect is dead, our rejected prince is missing, and once again, we have no leads."

"Oh, I didn't say that, Your Surliness." Byrnes clapped a hand on his shoulder. "Dead men don't talk. But you'd be amazed what you can learn about them if you do a little sleuthing. It seems our Guardsman Wallach was a bit of a gambler. Pockets too deep for his circumstances, so to speak. I've sent Ingrid and Lark out to do a little enquiring, but from what his fellow guards have mentioned, it seems Wallach was in debt. One guard recalls hearing a handful of dubious-looking gentlemen threatening to remove fingers if he didn't suddenly pay, and even offered to help him out. But three days ago, he was suddenly tossing coin in games again. Told my informant he no longer needed a loan."

Finally. "Please tell me you have a lead that isn't going to vanish on us."

Byrnes's smile widened. "We have a lead, and this time, I don't think it's going to vanish."

∽

"Your Grace."

Malloryn paused as Charlie caught up to him. "The prince?"

"Gone." Charlie's face wore a scowl. "He made it to the airfields before I could catch him. I don't know how much money he cast about him, but a Russian airship managed to depart despite the lack of paperwork."

Malloryn stilled. He'd thought Ivan innocent of any involvement in the assassination attempts, but why flee?

Mind racing, he turned to Charlie. "Just the prince? Or was his entire party with him?"

"Just the prince, and his man, Danil. The rest of the Russians are still in their chambers, and Herbert and Clara mentioned that the Grand Duchess is in a rage. Apparently, he informed her that the queen was likely to propose, and she... uh... destroyed everything."

"So she's unaware of the outcome of their conversation." Which meant Prince Ivan hadn't visited her since the queen dismissed his suit. "Ivan knows more than he should, but the rest of the party are merely dupes."

"As I surmised too, Your Grace."

A blonde woman had told the prince about the scarab brooches. A voluptuous blonde. At the time, Malloryn had assumed the prince was merely a decoy, but now?

It could have been a lie meant to distract Malloryn and his Rogues.

"Fetch me the Grand Duchess," he told Charlie. "Put her in the blue suite. I want to have a word with her."

Charlie winced. "She's a little scary, Your Grace."

Malloryn smiled. "So am I."

Though he doubted he'd have to threaten her. A woman scorned was more than likely to wish to strike at her ex-lover by any means possible.

He could almost feel the wheels turning.

He'd have a name by the end of the day. He knew it.

Sir Gideon's fingers twitched in Alexandra's hand.

She lifted her head from his bed sharply, her heart leaping into her throat. "Gideon?"

He stirred restlessly, his dark lashes flickering against his cheek, his tongue licking dry lips. His eyes began to slowly open.

By all the heavens! He was waking. "Don't move!" she told him sharply, reaching for the glass of water someone had left on his nightstand. "Here. Drink."

Tipping the glass to his lips, she nearly drowned him. Gideon sputtered, and Alexandra wore most of it as he started coughing and then couldn't stop.

"Good lord," he rasped, clapping a hand to his chest and looking down in surprise. "What happened? Why do I feel… like someone's cut me from… chin to navel?"

Perhaps because someone almost had. She hadn't been able to watch as Obsidian used a razor-sharp scalpel to slice into the sac of air that was crushing Gideon's lungs.

"Why?" she whispered. "Why did you do that?"

"Do what?"

"Push me aside so you—"

She couldn't say it.

Gideon collapsed back against the pillow as he gave a breathless laugh. "Because I would rather take a thousand bullets than see you catch… even one. I would die for you,

Alexa. I would be your shield when you have none. Always. Forever. No matter what may come."

Not "my queen," but "Alexa." Because she would always be a woman first in his eyes, and not a monarch.

The tears caught her by surprise.

Queens didn't have the luxury of crying. But though she caught the sob between her teeth, she could feel a tear sliding down her cheek.

No other man had ever been as true to her.

And the realization speared through her: she would love him. Always. Forever. And if she couldn't have him, then she would take no one else as husband.

Curse Malloryn. He would simply have to deal with her decision.

The queen's tears cleared as she leaned over Sir Gideon's bed and pressed her lips to his. "I will marry no other man than you," she whispered.

"Alexa!"

"No," she said firmly. "I love you. And with you by my side, we will be unstoppable. There is nothing I cannot handle with you in my life. And that is what a queen needs. A husband who is both stalwart and true. A husband who will not fear to tell her when she is wrong. A husband who will love her to the end of his days. A husband who is her very dearest friend."

Gideon tried to sit up. "Is this a marriage proposal? Or my queen's orders?"

"Both." Then she swallowed. "Unless you do not wish to marry me."

Gideon's thumb stroked the back of her hand. "I did not dare dream of such a thing. Nothing has changed, Alexa. I am still… unworthy."

"You were never unworthy," she said fiercely. "And we have changed this entire damned country. Why can we not change this one thing?"

He shook his head. "Malloryn is going to have an apoplectic fit."

Her heart skipped a beat. "Is that a yes?"

Again, he squeezed her hand. Then swallowed. "Yes. Yes. A thousand times yes. Though I fear I am being selfish."

"Never." A cry of relief escaped her, and she fell forward, resting her forehead on his shoulder. "I need you by my side. And Malloryn is simply going to have to deal with the fact that he does not control everything."

Gideon captured her hand. "Please tell me I can be there when you announce it."

Alexa kissed his cheek. "I promise."

CHAPTER 15

It was Byrnes and Kincaid who brought the crucial piece of information to him. Malloryn looked up from his desk, noticing the grins on both their faces. "Yes?"

"Who are your best agents?" Byrnes asked.

"Your favorite agents?" Kincaid added.

He glanced between them, then set his pen down. His afternoon with the Grand Duchess had proven merely another false lead, so he was desperately in need of some evidence. "My favorite agents are the ones who have found whoever wants to kill the queen."

Reaching inside his coat pocket, Byrnes produced a piece of paper with a flourish. "I have a receipt from the bank for a withdrawal for five thousand pounds, as paid to Guardsman Wallach."

Kincaid slammed another piece of paper on the desk. "And I have the prototype schematics for a particular type of drone that is designed to be unleashed on a field of war. A gyrfalcon, if you will believe. One of the mechs who escaped the Ironmonger enclaves created a pair of them for a customer he recognized from a very popular caricature that did the rounds several years ago. She thought if she didn't give him a name, then he'd never be able to trace her, but she didn't count on her notoriety."

"She?" He glanced at the receipt. And then the prototype schematics.

His eyebrows hit his hairline. And then he smiled.

Voluptuous blonde, indeed. Prince Ivan *had* been telling the truth.

"We've got her."

MALLORYN FOUND THE CULPRIT IN THE PORTRAIT GALLERY, staring at one of Queen Alexandra's forbears. Or perhaps, if he was being honest, she wasn't perusing the king himself, but the golden, shining crown upon his head.

"It wouldn't fit very well," he called, resting on his cane.

Princess Imogen almost leapt out of her skin, clapping a bejeweled hand to her substantial chest. "Good grief. *Malloryn*. Don't you have something to do rather than creeping around this bloody tower like a vulture?" Her lip curled. "Doesn't my cousin have some shoes that need kissing?"

Malloryn strolled closer, smiling a little. "I think she's a little busy at the moment, thinking about whose heads are going to roll for the near-death of her dear friend, Sir Gideon." He *tsked* under his breath. "The queen may have forgiven an assassination attempt upon herself, but Sir Gideon…. Well, I had to remind her that nobody has been hung, drawn, and quartered in centuries."

Princess Imogen paled. "O-of course. How… barbaric. Sir Gideon is well?"

"He'll recover, it seems. Though the queen's sense of mercy may not."

Princess Imogen blinked. "Have you found the assassin?"

"Yes. Though finding the assassin and finding the one

pulling the strings behind them have proven to be two different stories. However, my team has prevailed."

"Finding the one... behind the assassin?"

He had to hand it to her. She made an excellent production of being confused. "Someone clearly wanted the queen dead. They tried three times to have her killed. And I had to ask myself: why? It couldn't be a foreign power, hoping to destroy Britain's sense of equilibrium. Little would be gained, and most of the foreign envoys and princes were here to further their own interests. A dead queen grants them nothing.

"The old Echelon is dead, and the blue bloods who remain clamor that they're emphatically loyal to Her Majesty. They're already on probation, and know even the slightest provocation will part them with their heads. So, who has the most to gain from the queen's death? Her loss would throw Britain into chaos, unless there was someone else to step onto the throne. And that someone would most likely be your brother, Eugene."

"How dare you cast such aspersions?" Princess Imogen squared her shoulders. "Eugene had nothing to do with this far-fetched plot you claim."

"On that we agree. Eugene can barely tie his own shoes without supervision. He would be an excellent placeholder for some power behind the throne to manipulate."

There. A faint flicker of fear in her eyes.

"You made one fatal mistake, you know?"

Princess Imogen's eyes narrowed. "A mistake? What mistake?"

"It's a common occurrence among the nobility. They tend to think that servants are invisible, and carry on all manner of meetings in front of them." He shook his head. "And although fear is a powerful motivator, when one has spent decades treating the servants appallingly, it takes very little more than a promise of protection—say, from someone even more powerful—to draw a confession forth."

"What the hell are you talking about Malloryn?"

"Two of the undermaids recall seeing a magnificent brooch with similar scrollwork to this on your dresser. One of them claims you had several such trinkets in your jewelry box, and when I searched it this morning, I found this." He tossed a golden scarab beetle toward her. "It was created by a mech who served in the Ironmonger enclaves, by the name of MacGregor. You bought it a year ago because you thought it was regal, and it links you to an assassination."

Princess Imogen slapped the thing aside as if he'd thrown a ticking bomb at her. "How dare you enter my chambers? I should have you whipped. And that... that thing has nothing to do with me. I've never seen it before in my life!"

Malloryn smiled. "It's just a brooch. Is it not?"

She froze.

"Although," he drew the word out with relish, "according to Mr. MacGregor, you did have something to do with its inception. I had him view the court from one of the galleries an hour ago, and he pointed you out without a qualm. You ordered the scarab made two months ago. A gift for a rival, you told him, and he is willing to testify in court."

Princess Imogen hissed under her breath, tipping her chin high. "Is this some little plot you've formed, Malloryn? A way to cast such aspersions on my character and have me removed from court? You're not the only one with power, you know. I have friends in high places, and I shall see you flogged for this."

"I doubt it." Princess Imogen should have been a blue blood of the Echelon. She owned the same arrogance and sense of invulnerability. His smile slipped. "I'm not done yet, and I doubt even your friends can save you. I have a witness who saw you with the cook who slipped cyanide into the queen's honey cakes and cordial. I have your mech's confession. I have the boy you paid to deliver a rope to the dungeons so Guardsman Wallach could hang himself."

He tugged a small slip of paper from his coat pocket. "And this is a withdrawal slip from your bank. For the precise sum of five thousand pounds, which, conveniently enough, is the exact sum someone used to bribe Wallach. I can bury you in court with a half dozen witnesses. You are finished."

Princess Imogen moved to slap him, but he caught her wrist.

"You piece of filth," she hissed. "Unhand me! Servants? You think to use those unwashed ingrates to bring me down? You have nothing, Malloryn. You probably paid them yourself."

"Don't make another mistake," he warned her coldly. "You may be the queen's cousin, but I'm not certain she's feeling very fond of you at the moment. Besides…" He leaned closer, to enjoy playing the trump card. "I don't just have the servants in hand, you little bitch. I have Eugene too. Your dear little brother bleated like a lamb and told me everything."

"That idiot!" Princess Imogen tore at his grip. "It should have been me on the throne! The prince consort was courting *me* before Alexandra stole him away! He would have married me and put me on the throne, but she couldn't have that, could she? She took everything. She always took everything! My uncle spent years failing to have a child, and he finally managed to beget that sniveling little spawn on his bitch of a wife? Eugene was named his heir. And she stole it all!"

"By being born?" Malloryn shook his head. "You fool. You have riches, an estate, more than most people could possibly imagine—"

"The crown was ours! And it would have been ours again. I just had to take it! But she couldn't even have the good grace to die!"

There.

A confession.

Finally.

Malloryn let her go. "Thank you, Princess." He stepped aside as Sir Gregor strode out from the nearest drawing room, followed by a pair of guards. "Have you heard enough, Sir Gregor?"

Her Royal Highness gasped.

"Quite." The captain of the Coldrush Guards grabbed the princess by the arm, his expression one of loathing. "Your Highness, you may consider yourself under arrest for the attempted assassination of the queen."

"Malloryn!" she screamed, trying to throw herself at him and rake those nails down his face. "You bastard!"

He clasped both hands on the cane. "Enjoy your confinement, Your Highness. And your new notoriety. I'm going to make sure your likeness is plastered across every newspaper in London. Perhaps we'll use the Frogmore caricature, shall we? I believe that was your favorite, following your ill-fated rendezvous with the Spanish ambassador. You'll be the most famous woman in London."

Princess Imogen's snarls of rage echoed in his ears as she was dragged, rather unceremoniously, to her cell.

CHAPTER 16

The Duke of Malloryn climbed the tower slowly, rubbing at his knuckles. He'd dealt with the Imogen situation and then requested a private audience with the queen.

There were a thousand conversations he'd rather be having right now.

She'd been betrayed by almost everyone in her inner circle, and now her only remaining relatives had plotted to take the crown from her head. He felt a certain sense of pity.

At the top of the tower, the queen turned around with a whisk of her skirts. "Will it never end?" she demanded. "They stole my country from me and murdered my people. And when we finally won our freedom, they sought to cast me down. They burned my tower and tried to assassinate me again and again and again. And yesterday, a good man was nearly killed trying to save me! When will it end?"

"Your Majesty—"

"I mean it!" she cried. "I am done with these wretched plots. I am done being fair and benevolent to those who think to overthrow me. The blue bloods and the Echelon don't want me ruling over them? Then fine. I'll put them all in a bloody grave."

"Alexandra," he said, capturing her by the shoulders. "It wasn't a blue blood."

She froze. "Not a blue blood. Then who sent the guard? Who is behind this attempt? I want their head!"

Malloryn eased out a slow breath. "It appears we have a mole in the council chambers. It seems your cousin Imogen somehow heard we were considering naming Eugene as your heir, with a regency set in place. She sought to hasten matters and forestall a sudden marriage."

"*Imogen?*"

"Yes, your cousin Imogen. I believe she's been planning something like this for a while, as she'd ordered the brooch months ago."

The queen pressed her fingers to her temples. "No matter where I turn, there is always treachery."

"Not everywhere," he reminded her.

She shook her head. "I wish I had never been born to this life. I sometimes wish I was just a common woman out there on the streets of London."

"No, you don't," he said softly. "For those lowborn women have their own challenges, their own suffering. And you are the one who is in a position to do something about their lives."

The queen sighed. "I just wish this wasn't so complicated. And that Gideon…."

Her composure dropped, just for a second.

"Sir Gideon is safe," Malloryn assured her, squeezing her shoulders. "His wounds will heal."

"This time," she whispered. "He took a bullet for me."

"And he would do so again, if he saw another one coming."

"But I don't want that!" she cried. "I don't want to lose any of you."

"Any of us?" he asked gently. "Or mostly Sir Gideon?"

Faint circles of color crept into her cheeks. "I am fond of you all."

"But fondest of him, I think."

Their eyes met.

And perhaps it was time to reveal his cards. She'd suffered enough today, and as Adele had pointed out, sometimes he instinctively chose the more convoluted route when a simpler one would do.

"You should marry him."

She blinked. "Marry whom?"

"Sir Gideon," he said. Perhaps Adele had been right. Perhaps it was time for the games to end. "Forget the alliance. A foreign prince will never love you, nor you him. Not the way Sir Gideon would. And if you don't marry him, then you will always wonder at the life you could have had with him. You will always wonder what it feels like to love and to know love."

The queen's mouth dropped open.

"I.... You.... How did you...?"

He took pity on her. "What did you think this entire affair was all about? It was clear the pair of you held feelings for each other. I was merely trying to push one of you into taking action. You were wrong, Alexandra. Sir Gideon was my choice all along."

"You orchestrated this entire bloody husband hunt so I would finally act on my feelings for Sir Gideon?"

He shrugged. "I told you that you'd never guess which candidate I was backing. I told you it would be your choice."

The queen balled her fists. "I swear I should kick you off this tower! This is beyond the pale, Malloryn. Beyond!"

"Why?" he goaded her. "Because he's the one you want, and you hate it when I'm right?"

"I hate it when you always have to *be* right."

"I'm your spymaster. I wouldn't be doing my job if I

didn't have my finger on the pulse at all times. Marry him, Alexandra. Be happy. You deserve to be happy."

"Good God." She shook her head in disbelief. "Your wife has completely turned your life on its head, hasn't she?"

Malloryn drew back. "Well, of course, she has. But I don't see what that has to do with—"

"With you backing the sentimental choice?" she asked sweetly. "One year ago, you'd have never urged me to marry the man of my heart. You'd have been arguing about treaties and what is good for the country. You'd have been horrified I was even considering taking a human husband, when half the Echelon feels slighted following the revolution. You've changed, Malloryn."

Malloryn shut his mouth.

The queen looked delighted. "You've turned into a fairy godmother from some story. You're arranging marriages now. This is delightful."

"The realm *does* need an heir."

"Don't pretend to be so cynical. How many marriages have you arranged now?"

He shut his mouth again. Most of the Company of Rogues had managed to sort their own affairs, but Gemma had required a bit of convincing to accept Obsidian's proposal, believing marriage wasn't the sort of thing for a woman with her upbringing and skills. And there'd been the under-butler and one of the housemaids....

Dear God.

It was true.

He *had* turned into a fairy godmother.

Drawing himself up, he arched an icy brow. "Several. I arrange everything, including the dining table. And most importantly, the future heir of the kingdom."

"Speaking of heirs, Malloryn..., when *is* the baby due?"

His eyes narrowed. "Adele and I haven't discussed the possibility of such an event just yet."

The queen's eyes sparkled deviously. "I would suggest you discuss it, and soon, Malloryn. Your wife is positively glowing these days, and if she's not keeping a happy secret from you, then I will marry Sir Gideon and turn over all major decisions that involve the realm directly to you."

His heart skipped a beat. "With child? Adele with child?"

"Oh, I do enjoy knowing something you don't." The queen rolled her eyes. "I expect to be named godmother, Malloryn. Now go and find your wife. I'm sure you have some things to discuss." She brushed off her skirts, lifting her chin high. "And I have a certain knight to compromise."

M<small>ALLORYN FOUND</small> A<small>DELE IN THE MIDST OF A WHIRLWIND OF SILK</small> in her bedchambers.

Dismissing the maids with a look, he curled his arms around her from behind, rubbing his cheek against the back of her neck.

"Is there something you need to tell me?" he murmured.

Adele stilled. "What do you mean?"

He slid his hand down her abdomen and cupped a handful of fabric. He couldn't help capturing a breath. Hope had planted seeds in his heart, and he was half afraid he'd choke on them if she denied it.

Every inch of his wife went still, and then she punched him in the arm and escaped his grip.

"How?" she demanded.

It was true? A flutter of nerves overtook him. "Then you confirm it?"

"I was going to tell you. I just wanted… to be certain." Her voice dropped. "I didn't want to get my hopes up, but the midwives think I'm carrying well now."

He opened his arms, and she stepped into them.

Malloryn squeezed her tight and rested his chin on her head. "And they think it's safe now?"

"Yes," she said, in a small voice. "There's always a risk, but... They seemed very certain. And I've been so ill this time. It's a good sign."

They'd lost the first child they'd created, barely a week after Adele revealed the news to him. It had shattered her, and for the first time in his life, he hadn't known what to do.

Except hold her. And kiss her. And let her sleep in his arms after she'd cried herself to sleep.

The breath went out of him. He hadn't allowed himself to grow excited that first time, or to entertain thoughts of the child they'd share. But he couldn't defy the surge of hope he felt now.

Hauling her up into his arms, he carried her toward the bed.

Adele landed in the middle of the mattress with a squeak, but he gave her no time to protest. Instead, he captured the gasp on her lips and kissed her until they were both dizzy.

"Malloryn!" she gasped, arching her throat back to reveal it. "It's the middle of the day! What will the maids think?"

"That the duke adores his wife so completely that he's lost all notion of propriety these days," he said, returning his lips to her skin.

They lost themselves in each other, and he spent an inordinate amount of time kissing her belly before trailing his tongue lower.

Afterwards, they lay tangled in each other's arms. Malloryn idly stroked his fingers up and down his wife's back, enjoying the shiver that ran through her. "How was your day?"

"Hectic," she admitted, snuggling against him. "Lena's trying to prepare for her and Will's forthcoming trip to Stockholm for the Russian-Scandi summit. There's some sort of leadership squabble within the Scandinavian verwulfen clans, and she was a little concerned she was taking baby Alex into a verwulfen war. I said I may know someone who could provide some assistance for the embassy."

"Consider it sorted," he admitted. "Byrnes and Ingrid are going to be part of the ambassador's party. They'll keep an eye on things."

A hint of tension went out of her, and he realized she'd been worried about her friend. "Is that truly wise?"

"Byrnes and Ingrid? Of course. She's a little hotheaded, especially when it comes to verwulfen politics, but Byrnes is—"

He'd been about to say "cool and collected," but when it came to his wife, Byrnes had a bad habit of losing his head.

"I was speaking of Ingrid's injuries," Adele said.

They lay still for a moment.

"The nerves in her spine have healed, the doctors tell me," he said slowly. Ingrid had broken her back protecting Adele, and he didn't think he'd ever be able to repay her. Despite the veracity of the loupe virus, it had taken far longer than usual for Ingrid's shattered nerves to reknit, and months of hard work for her to walk again, let alone anything more stimulating. Byrnes had hovered over her the entire time.

"I would hate to see her progress stalled," Adele whispered. "Do you think it's a little soon? What if she's hurt again?"

The decision had vexed him for weeks. Ingrid and Byrnes were the perfect choice to infiltrate a verwulfen summit filled with both hotheaded warmongers who draped themselves in furs and carried axes, and the cold, vicious entourage of Russian blue bloods.

But he'd been there when Ingrid had forced herself to walk again.

He'd been the one she'd turned to when Byrnes wouldn't let her do anything more strenuous than a run.

And he'd seen the *need* in her eyes, when she'd picked up

her weapons and faced him in the practice ring, because some part of her had feared she'd never be able to fight again.

He'd been prepared to ease her into it gently, until Ingrid almost took his throat out.

"She needs this," he told Adele. "And I doubt she'll be placed directly in harm's way. Their task is purely to protect our ambassador and his wife. They're not to get involved in any Scandinavian politics or vengeful Blood Court assassinations. They're on protection duty only. And possibly my eyes and ears."

"I'm sure they won't involve themselves at all," she replied sweetly. "Byrnes and Ingrid following your orders? Absolutely. Without doubt. There will be no involvement in any mayhem. Nobody will die in mysterious circumstances. And Britain will definitely not have to deal with the complex political ramifications of the fallout."

He pinched her bottom. "That's why I'm sending the rest of them."

Adele squealed with laughter. Pressing a kiss to his throat, she stroked her fingers down his cheek. "How was the queen this morning?"

"Furious."

"Auvry—"

"I told her she had my blessings and that he was my choice all along," he said quickly, kissing her fingertips. "I thought about what you said, and perhaps you were right. She deserves a chance to be happy, and she looked so utterly miserable."

"How did she take such news?"

"She called me a 'fairy godmother,'" he admitted dryly. "She thinks I've taken a sudden penchant to arranging marriages."

Adele lifted her head off his chest, her eyes sparkling with delight. "Really?"

"Don't laugh," he told her in the most arrogant voice he

could summon. "I am the power behind the throne. Blue bloods cower when they hear my name. Mortals quiver at the sight of my house sigil. This is appalling."

Giggles spilled from her mouth. His lips twitched. Adele had a bad habit of snorting when she was overcome with laughter, and if anyone had told him a year ago that he'd find the sound adorable, he'd have insisted they were due a visit to Bedlam.

"Oh, Auvry." Straddling his hips, Adele planted her hands on his chest. "How terrible. I've ruined your reputation utterly."

He lifted up onto his elbows, tilting his mouth almost to hers. "Perhaps you should make it up to me?"

"With pleasure," she purred, then leaned down and captured his mouth in a possessive kiss.

Hours later, Malloryn made his way downstairs.

"Baby Ivy." Byrnes's voice echoed up the stairwell. "And I'm going to be the godfather."

Malloryn paused. He had babies on the brain. He could have sworn Byrnes had just placed a bet on the sex, name, and godparent of some unfortunate child.

Ava's confinement was fast approaching, but they'd already debated the matter, and he'd managed to get a glimpse of the betting book that Byrnes was keeping quiet from Kincaid. They wouldn't be speaking of it again, would they?

"Ivy?" Ingrid asked. "Why Ivy?"

"Because I like it."

"Who in their right mind would name you as godparent to their child?" Kincaid growled. "Christ. You'd probably give the little bugger a knife for its first birthday."

Kincaid.

His nostrils flared. Kincaid shouldn't be here for this conversation if they were speaking of Kincaid's child.

"You can never start them too early," Byrnes protested.

"A little boy," Charlie declared, and the sound of a pair of coins clinked as they landed on the table. "And Gemma will be the godmother."

Malloryn's brows drew together in a frown.

The others were all aware he viewed Gemma as some sort of... foster sibling. Surely not. Surely they couldn't be placing a wager on—

"I'll take you up on the sex of the baby," Byrnes said, "but not on the choice of godmother. Gemma's got it for sure."

"Unless the duchess chooses her dearest friend," Ingrid pointed out, "Mrs. Carver."

Malloryn's nostrils flared. Hell and bloody ashes.

"And Uncle Charlie is going to be godfather," Charlie added.

"That," Byrnes said, pointing at him, "is up for discussion. I'll take that bet."

The discussion grew livelier as they all debated the merits of this.

Malloryn had two options at this point.

He could quite thoroughly toss his crumpets and spew invective at the lot of them for presumably planting a listening device in his rooms, or he could ignore the violation and use it to his advantage.

Maybe toy with Byrnes a little, because he knew exactly which Rogue was the only one with the audacity to have planted such a device.

Malloryn sauntered down the stairs, arching his brow. "What on earth makes you think I'm going to allow any of you near my child, let alone name you godparents? Barrons is my closest friend. If I'm going to name anyone godfather, it's going to be him."

"*Yes*," Lark hissed, making a little celebratory fist.

Charlie rolled his eyes and flipped a pair of coins in her direction. "Congratulations, Your Grace."

A chorus of congratulations echoed around the table.

"I see there's a new betting book being opened," he said dryly. "If I find your listening devices, Byrnes, I will shove them down your throat."

"Listening devices?" Byrnes protested. "Why am I always the chief suspect?"

"Because you're always guilty."

"Not this time," Byrnes replied. He snorted and glanced toward Ingrid, who gave Malloryn a sweet smile.

"Your dear wife's been casting up her accounts several times a day," she replied. "She's also suddenly obsessed with cake."

"Adele is always obsessed with cake."

"Not like this," Ingrid said, looking impressed. "She asked Herbert to trot halfway across London in search of a particular honey cake she is absolutely fascinated with at the moment."

"And she eats it with cheese," Lark said with a shudder. "A foul sort of cheese that stinks the entire room out."

How on earth had they all known before he had?

Lark smiled sweetly at Malloryn, failing to wilt under his stare, as anyone with reasonable sense would.

He was clearly losing his touch. Fairy godmother. Arranging marriages. Now this.

Flipping out the end of his coat, he took his seat at the head of the table. "Herbert, fetch us some tea. I can see that none of us are quite busy enough. That's about to change."

"Very good, Your Grace." The butler vanished.

"You have a job for us?" Byrnes asked, rubbing his hands together.

"I have a job for some of you." Malloryn flipped a folder across the table toward Gemma. "Fancy a honeymoon?"

"I'm not even married yet."

"You will be," he replied. "And then you are going to be whisked away on an all-expenses paid voyage, complete with an entire new wardrobe and trousseau."

"Ooh," Gemma cooed, grabbing the folder. "You shouldn't have. Where are we going? Somewhere warm, preferably?"

"Morocco," Ingrid purred, closing her eyes as if imagining she was tilting her face toward the sun.

"Crete," Ava said brightly. "Imagine all those ruins!"

"It's going to be somewhere cold, dark, and bloody," Byrnes said sourly. "I only just ordered a new pair of boots after the last set were ruined in Russia."

"Yes," Malloryn said, "I noticed that invoice."

"They were ruined on your behalf, Your Grace."

He ignored the comment.

Because some wounds were still fresh enough to bleed, and he didn't particularly enjoy thinking of that period of time in his life.

"Stockholm," Gemma announced, her tone neutral. Her gaze lifted from the paper she was reading. "A diplomatic embassy to Stockholm, and we're to be included. This hardly sounds like our sort of thing."

"That's because you haven't read the entire report," he pointed out. "The queen is sending Will Carver, our verwulfen ambassador, to Stockholm to attend the renewal of the Treaty. It's been a hundred years since the Scandinavian verwulfen clans hammered out a treaty with the Russian Blood court about verwulfen clans in the Grand Duchy of Finland. The Russian court is sending a large contingent of princes to renew the treaty, and both the Norwegian and Swedish verwulfen clans will be in attendance."

"Sounds like the perfect stew of political mayhem," Kincaid muttered.

"Blue bloods and verwulfen clans," Gemma muttered. "My, my. It's going to be a bloodbath."

"It will be," he conceded. "The ambassador is to renew relations with the Scandinavian clans and foster a potential trade alliance with them. He is also there to witness the naming of the new War Hammer. I need for him to return alive and well. And not to break some Scandinavian verwulfen's nose."

Gemma winced. "That's possibly going to be the difficult part. Mr. Carver has a temper."

"You're in luck," Malloryn said. "His wife's going with him. And their son. Not only is he going to be on edge with all the social niceties, but his protective urges are going to be in full force." Malloryn smiled. "Imagine a volcano sent to parlay with a geographical faultline. And perhaps add in a bomb."

Gemma gave him a long, steady look. "I thought you said this could be my honeymoon?"

"What?" he mock gasped. "I've practically gift wrapped a present for you. You're bound to be shot at, at least once. Would you prefer taking in the waters somewhere? A nice, lazy sojourn to a cottage in Scotland?"

Gemma grimaced and clutched the folder tightly. "No. Being shot at is fine. Somewhat bracing for the nerves, but the aftermath is... extremely enjoyable." She gave Obsidian a saucy wink.

Malloryn pretended he didn't hear her. "Lark and Obsidian, this is also going to be somewhat of a family reunion. Your brother is reputed to be one of the Blood envoys."

They both blinked at him, then exchanged looks.

"Nikolai?" Lark said.

"Play nicely with him," he instructed. "I want a friend on the inside of the Blood court. There are rumors someone assassinated the tsarina's favorite grandchild as they all vie to be named heir, and Catherine is on her deathbed. Russia's more volatile than Will Carver right now. I want a prince in my pocket."

"Have you met Nikolai?" Lark asked bluntly. "'Nice' is not a word I'd use to describe him."

"Family trait, it seems," Malloryn murmured. "Kincaid, you and Ava are on retirement for a few months. Enjoy it. I'm sure I'll have need of both your services in the future." Stealing the folder back from Gemma, he graced them all with a smile. "Now go and pack. Something warm, I'd suggest. I believe the spring in Stockholm is... bracing."

"What about me?" Byrnes demanded.

"What about you?" he replied coolly as he pushed to his feet. "Someone has to mind the fort. And I'll need Herbert in the field for this one."

"Herbert?"

Malloryn examined his nails. "He has a certain level of diplomacy and subtlety you lack."

"He blew up an entire factory full of munitions!" Byrnes exploded.

"Your Grace," Ingrid said quietly.

Byrnes had earned it, but toying with Ingrid was beyond him. Malloryn tipped his head to her. "You're both on personal protection duty. I want the verwulfen ambassador and his family to return without a scratch on them, and who better to trust than the pair of you?"

A slow breath escaped her. "Thank you."

"Don't kill anyone," he said, directing the full attention of his gaze on Byrnes. "Don't insult anyone. Don't start any wars. Bring that big, hairy verwulfen bastard home to me in one piece, or I'll never hear the end of it from Adele. She is quite fond of Mrs. Carver."

"Why does everyone always look at me?" Byrnes protested.

"Cannot imagine," Kincaid growled.

Ava coughed into her fist, hiding a laugh.

Malloryn leaned back in his chair. "Well, what are you all

waiting for? The delegation leaves in five days. You have no time to waste."

"You're not coming with us?" Gemma asked, hovering above her chair.

Malloryn shook his head and laced his palms across his middle. "No. I just found out I'm going to be a father. I want to take Adele for a holiday to Bath, where we can take in the waters, lounge in bed, and she can eat cake and cheese until she's heartily sick of it. Neither of us have had a moment to think since the tower was destroyed. I want a holiday. And *I* want a honeymoon. Try not to completely destroy Britain's relations with two major European superpowers. I'll be very vexed if I have to return to London and commandeer a dirigible to rescue the lot of you."

Gemma granted him a curtsy and a devilish smile. "We wouldn't dream of it, Your Grace. We'll take care of everything. Two warring verwulfen countries bound by a treaty as thin as my corset laces, a scheming contingent of Russian blue bloods, and an ambassador who's not going to listen to anything we say. What could possibly go wrong?"

He winced. "That's why I'm sending Herbert. Dismissed."

EPILOGUE

LONDON STANDARD

The Queen and the Royal Family are delighted to announce that the Queen was safely delivered of a daughter on March 13, 1892. Her Royal Highness, Princess Charlotte Anne Henrietta, was born at 6:02 am today.

The baby weighs 9lbs 9oz.

The prince consort was present for the birth.

Her Majesty and her child are both doing well.

∼

BEFORE YOU LEAVE THE LONDON STEAMPUNK WORLD

Dear Reader,

EPILOGUE

Thank you so much for following this entire London Steampunk journey! I hope you enjoyed the queen's HEA—so many of you requested her story over the years that when it came time to sit down and write the epilogue, I simply couldn't look past her.

While this is the end of *London* Steampunk, you may have picked up a few hints of where this world is going next.

The good news? **London Steampunk: Blood Court** is officially on the schedule.

The bad news? Unless someone comes up with a way to clone me, it's not going to kick off until at least 2022, when **Legends of the Storm** wraps up.

For those who've followed me from the start and heard me mention my interest in the verwulfen clans in Scandinavia—I never really could work out how that series went, until a certain dark prince swaggered onto the page in **To Catch A Rogue**. So **Blood Court** will feature both the Scandinavian clans and the Court of Blood in Russia.

If you have read this epilogue novella without checking out the entire series, I hope you'll go back and see what you've missed. The Company of Rogues were such good fun to write that I would love to dabble with them forever—and one or two of them may make future appearances.

EPILOGUE

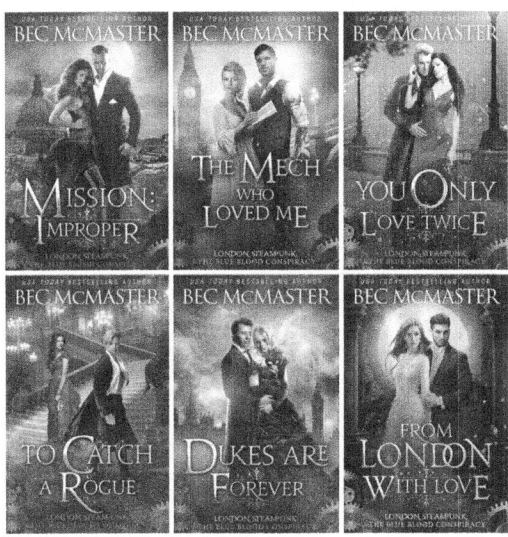

Available now:

Mission: Improper
The Mech Who Loved Me
You Only Love Twice
To Catch A Rogue
Dukes Are Forever

Want to make sure you don't miss any of the McMaster news?

Here are some other ways to stay updated:
* Follow me on Bookbub
* Visit my website at becmcmaster.com
*Or join my Facebook Fan Group for all the fun stuff, where I tend to be a little chattier!

I hope we meet again between the pages of another book!

EPILOGUE

Cheers,
Bec McMaster

LONDON STEAMPUNK
ROYAL FAMILY

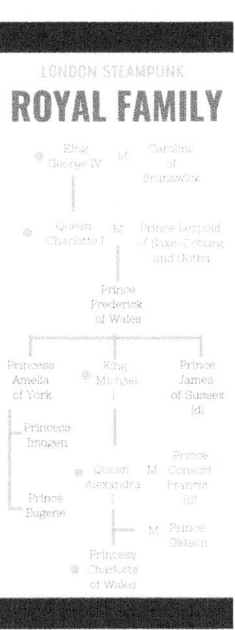

London Steampunk was written in an alternate timeline, from which history diverged at a certain point.

Avid history buffs may note that Princess Charlotte, the beloved wife of Prince Leopold, died in childbirth (with the child) in our real timeline—therefore giving rise to Queen Victoria's reign.

In the London Steampunk world, I like to pretend that she survived the birth along with the child—though due to complications, little Prince Frederick was the only child "Queen Charlotte I" would have had.

This is how Queen Alexandra I came to be, and the rest, as they say, is history.

ALSO BY BEC MCMASTER

DARK COURT RISING

Promise of Darkness

LEGENDS OF THE STORM SERIES

Heart Of Fire

Storm of Desire

Clash of Storms

COURT OF DREAMS SAGA

Thief of Dreams

LONDON STEAMPUNK SERIES

Kiss Of Steel

Heart Of Iron

My Lady Quicksilver

Forged By Desire

Of Silk And Steam

Novellas in same series:

Tarnished Knight

The Clockwork Menace

LONDON STEAMPUNK: THE BLUE BLOOD CONSPIRACY

Mission: Improper

The Mech Who Loved Me

You Only Love Twice

To Catch A Rogue

Dukes Are Forever

DARK ARTS SERIES

Shadowbound

Hexbound

Soulbound

BURNED LANDS SERIES

Nobody's Hero

The Last True Hero

The Hero Within

SHORT STORIES

The Many Lives Of Hadley Monroe

Burn Bright

ABOUT THE AUTHOR

BEC MCMASTER is a writer, a dreamer, and a travel addict. If she's not sitting in front of the computer, she's probably plotting her next overseas trip, and hopes to see the whole world, whether it's by paper, plane, or imagination.

Bec grew up on a steady diet of '80s fantasy movies like *Ladyhawke*, *Labyrinth*, and *The Princess Bride*, and loves creating epic, fantasy-fueled romances where even the darkest hero can find love. She lives in Australia with her very own hero, and her daughter.

Read more at www.becmcmaster.com

THE END

AFTERWORD

This book is for Baby McMaster, who I never got to meet—and for all those other little angel babies out there. You are never forgotten.

I owe huge thanks to Olivia Ventura, my editor, who painted red all over this manuscript, and then helped me nail down the precise title Princess Imogen would have.

To Jennie Kew, Nina Deal and Danielle Rowlands for the beta read—sometimes it's hard to see the forest for the trees, and you all pointed out elements that needed tightening.

To the creative team at Damonza for the cover. You blew my mind this time round. Also: Sir Gideon is hawt.

To my Facebook Fan Group, who helped choose the royal baby's name!

And last, but certainly not least: To my readers. Each and every one of you who has supported me on this journey and made London Steampunk what it is.

This one is for you.